D0254801

Get Up Girl! YOU GOT THIS!

How to Rise From The Ashes of Abuse

Brandie Dixon

Dedication

I dedicate this book to my mother, Penny Dixon, who has given me the strength of who I am today. She has stuck by me from beginning to end. We have cried together and laughed as well. She is my best friend, and although I have endured a lot of brokenness, saw her struggle and rise above her own abuse and inner being has given me the strength to write and empower other women and give them hope that it can change if you allow it.

To my husband, Carl Robinson III, I love you so much. Thank you for being my best friend and such a great supporter. It means the world to me to have you by my side as I dream of helping others overcome.

To my children, my crew, Destiny, Anthony, and Kay'Lynn, you have been the wind beneath my wings. We have gone through so much but here we are on the other side of it all. I thank God for the three of you and I am excited to see how bright you all shine now and in the future. I love you so much.

I also dedicate this book to a very good friend who believed in me and motivated me to never give up and always keep trying. I look up to her, and without her courage and bravery, I would not be able to share my story. I have cheated death, and the enemy has tried to end my life, but with her perseverance for me, I am strong. I love you, Anna Marie Jackson, and you are the sister I never had.

I also would like to dedicate my book to the one person who gave me the strength to write, advice, and resources to get this done. Without you, I promise, I would probably be that scared little girl still looking for answers to my struggles. Thank You, Jasmine Branford.

Acknowledgements

To *Donna Ivey*, thanks for being there for me when I really needed you. I appreciate you so much. *Teressa Chambers*, words cannot express how grateful I am for your kindness and generosity. Thank you so much for being there for me through my journey. *Alana Dixon*, thanks for all your help and encouragement. *Sharnell Quintyne*, your words of encouragement inspired me during a difficult time. You'll never know how much your help meant to me. Thank you.

To *Douglas Gallagher*, *Joanne Schilk*, *Tiffany Pearson*, and *Frances Jackson,* I will always remember your kindness and support. Thank you very much! *Julia Williams*, I just wanted to write to let you know how much I appreciate the positive influence you've had on my life. Thank you for your concern and useful advice! I'll be forever grateful. *LaTonya Cantrell*, thanks for helping me! You're the best!

To *Teneshia Anderson*, please accept this thank you as a small token of appreciation for the support you've given me. Your kindness means so much to me. *Tiya Riggins*, I just wanted to let you know how much I appreciate your support. Thank you for being there for me. You know I'd do the same for you in a heartbeat!

To *Sharea Mcphaul*, you are a blessing to me, and I will always remember your kindness. *Mike and Deborah Alford*, your positivity and kindness have made an unbearable time a little bit better. I didn't think that was possible, but I should have known better than to underestimate you! Thank you for sharing your light. The world is a better place, and I am a better person for it. *Kyasia Archer*, life has definitely been trial and error but having you in my life and us talking and you encouraging me and me encouraging has been very uplifting to get through my struggles and I thank you for being a good friend.

To *Natashia Jones*, thank you for always being there for me when I need you! *Shasta Edwards*, you are a wonderful friend, and I appreciate your love, kindness, support, and generosity. Thank you for always being there for me when I need you! *Vanetra Reese*, you are such a light! Thank you for brightening my view when all I could see was darkness. You are such a special person, and I am so incredibly lucky to call you, my friend.

To **Chontelle Matthews**, please accept my warmest thanks for your thoughtfulness and words of comfort. I appreciate you more than words can say. **Rashonda Fretwell**, **Brenda Mainor**, and **Sarah Rolley**, thanks for all your help and encouragement. **Karen Franklin**, your words of encouragement inspired me during a difficult time. You'll never know how much your help meant to me. Thank you. **Azgene Sconiers**, words are not enough to express to you how grateful I am for your help, so I will simply say thank you. I only hope I'll be able to return the favor sometime. If there's ever anything you need, all you have to do is ask!

To **Sharon McCoy**, thanks for all your help and encouragement. You make me feel seen and heard, and I love you for that. I hope you know how special you are to me. **Gabrielle Garrett**, you couldn't have shown up at a better time. Thank you for your support! **ZeEster Browning**, words cannot express how grateful I am for your help. You were there for me when I needed it the most. Thank you for everything that you've done for me. **Dena Helfrich**, you are a wonderful friend, and I appreciate your love, kindness, support, and generosity. Thank you for always being there for me when I need you!

To **Keely Dillon**, you cannot imagine how much strength your support has given me during this difficult time. Thank you for your thoughtfulness and your words of encouragement. **TaJana Kamin**, you never fail to make me smile. Thanks so much for your help and support! **Abby Dixon**, thanks for all your help and encouragement and being the best Uncle. **Jaycee Collins**, you are such a generous, kind person. Thank you for all your help!

To The One Who Changed My Life Forever,

This letter, I know, is another vain attempt to master the chaos within me. It is hard to put into words all that you put me through. But trying is always a better option than quitting. Sometimes I wish you could go through the pain and struggle you put me through, but really, I know there's no way I'd want another woman to go through the abuse I've endured. I've held onto this pain for so many years because I genuinely believed that someday it would stop. I always believed that my abusers were something more than they had appeared to be, but they were just like everyone else who caused me pain. Eventually, the past and you took advantage of my innocence until you eventually destroyed me completely. You thought you were powerful because you played an attacker. You thought I was weak because I played a victim. The truth is your victim is always superior to you in every way.

I would be lying if I told you I never thought about revenge. My hate for you surpasses anything you can possibly imagine. You are selfish, dishonest, controlling, manipulative, and messed up in the head. The ways you treated me, and the things you did to me when you were still a part of my life, were not what any true man would ever do. You made me believe that I could never trust anyone and that everyone would hurt me. You made me believe that I was never good enough. You tried to convince me that you were a good man; you were not. You warped my mind and imposed your own narcissistic views upon me. I never learned how to be a woman in a healthy, intimate relationship. You made me feel like I could never stand up for myself. You were more than imperfect. You were evil and toxic. I may have been abused by you, but was not, am not, and I never will be you.

My mind wandered, but my demons never got the best of me. Maybe I was simply too young to retaliate, or maybe I was too wise. I knew that if I were to sink to your level, you and I would be no different. One thing I've known for sure for all these years is that I never want to become a reflection of you or any of the people who have hurt me. I've always wondered to myself, "Do people always do these things to the ones they love?" I've thought, then, that maybe I just don't know enough about love.

You would always make an excuse of why you felt it was okay to abuse me. Over time, I started to believe the fault was in me. But today, I choose to stop blaming myself. It was never my fault to begin with. Nothing I said or did made it okay for you to hurt me with your words or your fists. I am not an excuse for your incapability to control your emotions. I am not the cause of your outbursts. I am not your rage or your hate. I am not your false pride or fragile ego. I am not the weakness you always claimed to see in me. I am not the names you called me. You don't define me. I define myself. I am much more than the marks you've left on my body.

I am innocence. I am dreams. I am hope. I am forgiveness. I am the person others always want to have around because I am laughter, and I am love. I hope the scars on my heart heal faster than the ones on my body. But the wounds within you, whatever caused them, I hope they heal even faster than mine. And when that day comes, I will be long gone from your life, and it will be too late to reach out to me to tell me that you're sorry. But today, I forgive you because today I want to be free.

From,

The Heart Of A Woman Whose Life You Changed Forever

Introduction

Notes To A Girlfriend

Hey Girl,

This book will serve as a conversation between girlfriends. I know that what you are experiencing or have experienced is heavy, heavy stuff. I know that it has been the worst thing ever, and it feels like the toughest thing to get through. However, I am someone who has been there and done that. Because this is true, I want to lend you my story in a series of short notes as a point of empowerment to help you make a decision. What decision is that Brandie, you may ask? Well, the decision to GET UP! Girl, you have what it takes, and I want you to see this as your truth.

These notes are my way of showing you that if I can get up, so can you. So read each one as a separate conversation between us where I share with you my personal truths, woes, heartaches, and even triumphs. I've thrown in some encouragement notes too so that you will know where you can begin to take your life back. At the end of this book, I have left space for you to write a few notes as well. As you are writing think of it as you are sending a note to me, your girlfriend. It will be your safe place to unload.

So, I can think back to being alone and by myself and thinking, should I tell my story? Who would be impacted, and what if my truth, my real-life story could cause harm instead of good? I had to realize that telling my truth could affect the people I had loved my whole life for over decades but knowing that telling the truth and breaking the silence would help me and those around me, helped me to decide. I had to learn that it's not my responsibility to protect the abuser. Keeping silent my whole life has caused me to be on an emotional rollercoaster and have the disorders I have been diagnosed with. PTSD, anxiety, and depression have gripped me because of what I have endured. I am sure that you may be able to relate to some of those. But as we journey through this healing, we will be sure to overcome by being truthful with self first. With that, I will share my story in hopes that you will be empowered to seek change or be completely healed and not surface healed.

"When we own the story, we can write a brave new ending."
- Brene Brown

One of the things I've learned is that feeling broken does not mean that you should just give up. However, it does mean that you need to take a step back and let those feelings come to the surface. We all feel broken from time to time, and we all have endured some level of hurt and pain from our past experiences. These are things that we can choose to put towards life to get better and focus on the positive and move forward. Like many people, I've always believed that a relationship with abuse was one in which there was only physical abuse, like slapping, hitting, or kicking. I didn't realize that a relationship was also abusive if one partner bullied, threatened, manipulated, or neglected the other. The way that one speaks, using a particular look, etc., can be abusive as well.

Did you realize that most abusers feel powerless? They don't act insecure by covering up this truth, but it is true. They feel powerless so they create a false since of power by becoming bullies. The one thing they all have in common is that their motive is to have power over their victim. This is the personal power they feel they lack. They can be amazingly successful in worldly ways, but not within. To them, communication is a win-lose game. The abuser always feels insecure, needy with unrealistic expectations of a relationship, distrustful, and often jealous. They can be verbally abusive, feel the need to be right and in control, and also very possessive. The abuser may try to isolate their partner from friends and family, be hypersensitive, react aggressively, and, more than likely, have a history of aggression. Many things can be associated with an abuser. Their feelings of powerlessness, however, leave their partners feeling broken beyond what they feel is repairable.

I want you, for a second, to recognize what being broken can mean for you or others. We may think that life itself has lost its meaning, and more likely than not, something has hurt us to the point that everything we touch seems tainted. We feel that no one can be trusted, and everyone is evil. Once we experience this in our lives, we pretty much feel that life has no value. Everything seems corrupted. This is the reason why we emotionally detach from others around us during and long after this time of abuse. We even shut down and block out the world as a whole. It gets to the point, at times, where we feel nothing can hurt us because nothing around us matters anymore. Numbness becomes a big part of our norm.

When these things happen to us, we are not free of pain but just building a wall from it. We isolate ourselves until it becomes easier not to speak and create this unspoken hope that the world will forget about us. The feeling of being broken robs us of our ability to enjoy anything in life. In our minds, we have built this no love, no hope, no trust, no loyalty wall. Even friendships become lies, and nothing can make us believe it will be different.

So, girlfriend, listen, if you've experienced abuse, it's essential to get support and learn how to set limits. Abusers deny or minimize the problem, as do victims who claim that their abusers can't control themselves. This is untrue in most cases. Many abusers also blame their actions on us, implying that we, the victims, are the ones that need to change.

Say this with me: "I am never responsible for someone else's behavior." If you don't remember anything else, remember that part. We cannot have you walking around feeling that everything that goes wrong or every reaction or response is on you.

And guess what? Yes! I say those same words to myself. I'm learning to stand up for myself again. I'm thankful that I walked away when I did because so many victims of emotional abuse can't see they're being hurt and end up emotionally damaged. During this recovery period, I'm slowly beginning to understand the sort of man I deserve. I'm also learning a lot about myself – my strengths, worth, and what I can bring to my next relationship. As you read through the pages of my story, I want you to begin to search for those same things in yourself. We are overcomers! We are going to rise from these ashes because they will not define us forever.

Remember this Girlfriend:

"By not confronting abuse to avoid the risk of losing someone's love, you risk losing yourself."

Here's to our complete and total healing,
Brandie

Note #1

Abuse is real!

Let me tell you something. Some people think they were not abused as children because they were never hospitalized, it only happened once, their partners did not mean it or did not know any better, or other people had it much worse than they did. They have never been more wrong. The after-effects can show up immediately, but a lot of times, it shows up later in life thus, it is not recognized for what it is. This is why I feel that I am here to tell my story and tell my truth of childhood abuse, being raped at 15, being emotionally abused, and physically abused. It took me a long time to get to this point because abuse in one's past is difficult to admit to. Many of you may never have made the connection between what happened to you as a child or even as an adult, but I am here to be that voice for you, to help you recognize that it wasn't all in your head. You felt it and knew that something wasn't right, and that's probably what drew you here to read this book.

Being in an abusive relationship, I learned to recognize some things. It was a cycle that took place. It goes like this: A build-up of tension, the attack, remorse and apology, and a honeymoon period of loving gestures right before it happened again and again. Do you recognize this from your life at all? There's often some sort of threat that goes with it, and sometimes the threat of abuse is all the abuser needs to control you, like a terrorist. Once the pattern reveals itself, though, the best time to abort abuse is in the build-up stage. It happens so often for some and in the same cycle that some victims will even provoke an attack to get it over with because their anxiety and fear are so great. These cycles cause you to be on edge and to feel like you must stay walking on eggshells. If you have seen or remember this happening, then it is a sign that you have experienced or are experiencing abuse.

Here is something else, after an attack, abusers say how sorry they are and promise never to repeat it. But without counseling to treat the underlying triggers of the abusive behavior, it will repeat itself. There's not really anything to stop it. Do not believe their promises. This is why it is so critical to avoid getting involved with an abuser when you're dating. To do this, beware of someone who: insists on having his or her way and won't compromise, has outbursts of anger, is rude to others, criticizes you or your family, is jealous or possessive, is paranoid and threatens you all the time. Pay attention to these signs even though the person is pursuing you and expressing love and affection. An abuser won't risk becoming abusive until he or she is confident that you won't leave. Think about this truth very hard. Don't stress it but be mindful of it from this day forward.

Take notice of a few other things as well. It is very likely that they will try to win you over and isolate you from friends and family. Check to see if they respect your boundaries too. Often, violence doesn't start until after marriage or the birth of a child, when you're less likely to leave them. But it can also escalate when you make the right choice and try to get yourself out. This is why it's imperative to have a plan and support.

Abusers can have a Jekyll and Hyde personality, which will confuse the hell out of you if you are not constantly paying attention. You will not know if you are going or coming. Dr. Jekyll is often charming and romantic, perhaps successful, and makes pronouncements of love often. You love Dr. Jekyll and make excuses for Mr. Hyde because of that love. You may not see the whole person, and this is the problem. If you've had a painful relationship with a parent growing up, you can confuse love and pain. I eventually realized that in the abusive relationship, I was allowing myself to go through it all. All I know now is that abuse is, indeed, real, and we can't continue to live as if it is not.

What did the abuse tell me about myself or how the world works for other women and me? What is the truth? I learned that we women often stay because they do not have the finances, nowhere else to live, no outside emotional support, childcare concerns, they're taking the blame for the abuse, denying, minimizing, and rationalizing the abuse, have low self-esteem, and confidence and they will always love the abuser, no matter what. When you're a victim of abuse, you feel ashamed. You've been humiliated, and your self-esteem and confidence have been undermined. You hide the abuse from people close to you, often to protect the reputation of the abuser, and you do this because of your own shame. Girl!!! I know it. It feels like the secret that should be your best-kept one. Shame holds on when abuse has played its part.

Here is something else that helped me to recognize the realness of it all. An abuser uses tactics to isolate you from friends and loved ones by criticizing them and making remarks designed to force you to take sides. You're either for them or against them. If the abuser feels slighted, then you have to take their side, or you're befriending the enemy. It's so sad, but it's so true. And it's designed to increase control over you and create your dependence upon them.

SN: This is why it's essential to build outside resources and talk about what's going on in your relationship. I do not mean in a gossipy way that undercovers your home business to anyone who will listen, I am speaking of a professional being the best person because you can build your self-esteem and learn how to help yourself without feeling judged or rushed into taking action. If you can't afford private therapy, find a low-fee clinician in your city, learn all you can from books and online resources, join online forums, get a life coach that specializes in healing from abuse, and find a support group at a local battered women's shelter. Do this even if it means keeping a secret. You're entitled to your privacy. Just start somewhere that will lead you from being in denial that it has or is happening to being able to live free once again. Girlfriend! I know you can do this. Take this step.

As you continue to journey into my world of abuse, you will see that I clearly had to follow my own steps to get me out as well.

Note #2

Life Was No Picture Book!

Now, I didn't always remember my abuse, well, at least not consciously. I repressed most of it until I was an adult. I blocked out almost all my childhood. I lived my life through photo albums of our family. I made up stories to go with the pictures, and I believed those stories were true. In my early 20s, I began having suppressed memories come back to me. I began to realize the stories of those pictures in the photo albums weren't true. My childhood, in reality, was a far darker place. My mind protected my heart through those pictures, so I wouldn't know what was really happening. My mind blocked the reality. Isn't that something? I was so used to seeing life through the fantasies I created through pictures. Now I know that life was not a picture book. This was a hard and harsh reality. When the memories returned, they felt like dreams. It was like seeing them through a wall of water or heavy mist. Even though I forgot most of my abuse, there were a few things that I never forgot. I just sort of stuffed them away and covered them with my created reality.

A part of the abuse that I pushed back was sexual. I didn't define it as sexually abusive until I learned the true definition of what that was. I minimized the encounters by just calling them "strange" and "hurtful." I had always remembered some of it, though I thought those things were just normal. That didn't prove that my recovered memories were real either, but they do show me that my family was sexual abusers and not the family I thought I had. I felt terribly alone, no matter how many people were in my life. It was the neighbor's house where I was sexually abused, and it came up in my mind all the time. When I would drive by the house or even the exit of the highway. It was them that I considered family, so the recollection messed me up big time. I was hurting while remembering.

I had implicit memory (emotional and physical reactions) before I'd consciously remember an abusive event. Days beforehand, I'd feel gloomy or find myself craving chocolate or using some other coping method. I didn't only have recalled memories; I had body memories. On one occasion, when a friend was helping me with a floor exercise, she grabbed my leg to position it correctly. When she touched me, I shrieked and scrambled away from her, and then I burst out in tears. I flashed on someone positioning me for better "access." But the same way I felt it in my body, there were times when I felt I wasn't even in my body. It was hard to accept those things as real, but they kept coming up. All of them seemed to have a common theme of betrayal and violation. As hard as it was to accept, it was hard to deny that they gave some explanation to all that I'd felt my whole life, the ways I thought and behaved. When the memories started coming up, I wanted to dismiss them, but I also desperately wanted to break through the fog. I was afraid of what I was seeing, but I was more afraid of not knowing. I hated believing something might be there, yet not be able to see it clearly or at all.

I'd accept my memories as valid one day and deny them the next. But there was something about them that felt true, and I couldn't shake the relief I felt that there were answers to those strange behaviors and feelings. My memories surfaced slowly over several years. I think them coming any faster would have overwhelmed me and left me too weak to actually process them. That's the point of remembering, as far as my healing is concerned. It's not so much about what happened; it's about how it affected me and properly allowing the emotional cuts and bruises to get some air and appropriate care. I know now that healing can't take place without the correct care.

When I was being abused, I couldn't stop it, but I used what resources I could to help me survive. One of those resources was to repress the memories. Just as I used the resources available to me during my abuse, I used what I had available to heal. I believe every abuse survivor has the same ability to heal when they realize that, yes, they have been abused and when they decide they are truly ready. Before I had specific memories, I started to heal with what I had. I worked on boundary issues and on affirming my value apart from sex. I used what I knew. Looking back on my healing journey, most of the healing has come from the emotional abuse, not specifically the sexual abuse. If I'd understood then how much I'd been abused in other ways, I could have made huge progress in my process without even recovering one sexual abuse memory. The thing that bothered me was that I used those details like what color the wallpaper was to "prove" that I really remembered my abuse correctly because it was so hard to accept. But those details don't really matter when it comes to healing. I didn't need to know how old I was or which bedroom it happened in. The only thing that mattered when I was sorting those things out was what that event told me about myself. What false messages did I learn that I needed to debunk? Seeing the truth isn't about the color of the walls; it's about seeing that I'm a valuable person no matter how I was treated.

It's been difficult having to face the memories that resurfaced. The reality vs. the picture book life was awful, yet the biggest reason I believe in my memories is that my life is completely different since I've been using them to heal. As I've addressed my past, I've been on the journey to healing my life.

Note #3

Let me tell my truth!

Over the years, abuse found me, and I was helpless to it, so I thought. Childhood abuse was only the beginning. I would later walk into a situation that would indeed change me. I thought I met the best man ever — this man who would eventually identify as a drug user of cocaine and as an alcoholic. He was very abusive to me mentally, physically, verbally, and spiritually.

I can remember him choking me in a car while pregnant with my unborn son. At that moment, I was thinking, "what man could ever harm the mother of his child?" I stayed and went through more abuse because of many of the reasons that I gave before.

Like many women, even after that, I still loved him! My heart kept screaming at me not to leave him. Yes, even after he almost killed me. If you're lucky, your head will start to outweigh your heart. You'll stop denying that this person is no good for you. Finally, you'll dig deep and find the courage to walk away. I did. But not before going back to him many, many times. The drug-like pull back toward him was so great. After we first reunited again, the high was better than the pain I felt when I was without him, alone. When you leave an abusive person, the withdrawal feels as agonizing as I imagine it might be weaning off heroin. It did for me, at least. You've been numb for so long that a gamut of emotions pours out at once. Shame, anger, loneliness, guilt—you name it, you feel it. It hurts. I have never sobbed like that before in my life. I was so overwhelmed by their rawness. But you need to feel these emotions, as painful as they are. You need to thaw out. To go cold turkey to recover.

Unless you look hard at why you were addicted to an unavailable person in the first place, you risk going back to them—or replacing them with a different drug, in the form of another abusive person. Either way, like any addict, you risk losing your life. I had to ask myself the same difficult questions others asked me. Why is it I still love someone who abuses me? Why is it I need to numb myself with someone who is like a drug to me? Someone you know is no good for you but is the only thing that will make you feel good again. Hopefully, like me, you'll realize your addiction started way before you ever met this person. I'm sure you know already that it has something to do with low self-esteem. If we don't love ourselves, we're attracted to those who treat us as though we are unlovable. But it's not enough to just tell someone they need to "love themselves more." "I knew deep down I needed to work on my self-esteem!" But trust me, that's easier said than done. Believe me.

It hurts. Every night I cry myself to sleep because I can feel the weight of my hurt and my pain compressing on my chest. I feel lonely and uncared for. All I've ever wanted was to find my happiness. That's why I share my story to let you know, whoever you are, that you're not alone. I feel it, too, the sadness and the wanting to be left alone. The random bursts of anger you get because you don't know how to control your emotions. The self-hatred and self-loathing. The need to just disappear. The desire to just stop feeling. You want to get out of your comfort zone, but you can't because, again, you're afraid. I know that feeling too. I know it all too well.

Note #4

My Daddy Hurt Us!

I've laid agonizing over my pain from abuse and thinking back, recalling that my father abused my mother before I was five years old. My brother and I were lying in a ditch one cold night because daddy was inside hurting mommy. I am not sure that I fully grasped what was happening at the time, but I remember my mom packing me and my brother up and us driving and driving, not knowing where we were going. In a blink of an eye, daddy was gone, and we would probably never see him again. Because I couldn't fully understand it, I was so confused with why mommy had to leave and why we were being taken away from my father. Will I ever get the chance to talk with him? Will he be here for my recitals, graduation, or even one day walking me down the aisle? How could the perfect family go wrong?

Nothing was making sense to me if I can be honest. I knew that I didn't like hearing my mother get hurt, but I was also used to seeing my dad on a regular basis. But one day, my mother got tired of it all, and she couldn't take the abuse anymore. She had dealt with so much over the past 16 plus years. From being stabbed, thrown downstairs, punched in the stomach, slapped, kicked, and mentally and emotionally battered. She reached out to close family in Georgia, and when he was away in jail for a couple of days, she packed up everything she could and put us in her car, and we drove all the way to Georgia to start our lives over. It's crazy to find out the full story about someone else's abuse. It's sad to consider that it really goes that far. In this case, it was even more real because these were the people that I loved that I was given as parents.

He was abusive toward my mother, but I still loved him just as I loved her. How does that work exactly? At such a young age, all I knew was that he was missing. I wanted my father in my life even though I knew that what he was doing to my mommy was wrong. That's a part of what confused me so much.

I guess I fixed my mind to think that I wouldn't have gone through a lot of the abuse I endured if he had been there. I yearned for my father's love and wanted him in my life so badly, but I had to accept that the abuse my mother went through wasn't deserved, and she needed to be happy and safe enough to move forward in her own life. My father has been in but mostly out of my life ever since I was a child. I didn't fall apart. I managed. But I always wondered what it would have been like if things had been different. What if he had made a better choice so that he didn't have to be left behind?

I was daddy's little girl, or was I? I was trying to understand why, if my father loved us and my mom, we had to leave? Why wouldn't I be able to see him anymore? Although I was doing just fine without him, I'd always catch myself imagining his presence during important times in my life. I was the lucky one who got to ride his back, and daddy would teach me how to make pizza every week. I was the one who got to walk to the dam every weekend and go fishing. We had the perfect life, and where did it go wrong? Like most people who grew up without a father, I turned out OK. My life wasn't completely ruined by his absence, but every now and then, I sensed the empty space that he could have filled. I always said I didn't need him, and I was fine without him in my life.

One day, someone asked me what I would say to my dad if I wrote him a letter. I thought this question was easy to answer. I would tell him he missed out. And I'd tell him that I never needed him in the first place. I'd tell him everything is fine even though I haven't seen him in a long time. There are just some things that we can't understand no matter how hard we try. I couldn't write to him based on what I didn't know, but I would express what I did. I'd say...

Dear Daddy,

I forgive you for never being by my side and for abandoning me without explanation. You should know that the pain of not having my father there for me has made me a stronger woman. Thanks to you, I know how to get through difficult situations on my own. You crossed my mind out of the blue today. Instead of feeling rage, heartache, or hate, I found myself smiling a little. Not because of you, though, but because of me. I am a fatherless daughter that survived your failure.

Even though the void left by an absent father is hard to fill, I forgive you. It's helped me to value those who have stepped up to take your place. My Aunt, my grandmother, and of course, my mother. She's been my faithful companion all this time. She has photos and memories of my childhood that you aren't in. She's been there during every stage of my life, and she's proud of the memories we've created. She taught me what true love really is.

I forgive the fact that you made innocent people play the role of father and grandparent at the same time. I hope you can truly understand the mental and emotional effects this has caused on my brother, and I hope you will forgive yourself for not being there for us. I miss you so much, and it's hard for me to say it, but it's true. Even though I've grown up and I'm doing all right, I always felt like something was missing. And I still do. I know that everyone makes mistakes. And some mistakes lead you to places you never meant to go. Some mistakes turn you into someone you never wanted to be. But it's not too late, Dad.

Genuinely Spoken,
Brandie

Note #5

I Thought I Was Safe!

At age eight, I was friends with so many of the neighborhood kids, I felt my life was somewhat good. I had those friends, and I could play outside, spend the night out, and attend parties. I was mostly happy with life, and then the worst thing happened.

One night mommy said I could spend the night with my best friend. Her family was the best family ever in my eyes. The mother had eight kids and what I saw from a child's eyes was the perfect family. Their father was a deacon in the church and, to me, was the best neighborhood dad ever. He was a great father because he had eights kids, and he still treated me and my brother as if we were his own, and he felt like the father I never had.

We would have social gatherings, play baseball, and attend church every Sunday and Wednesday. It was so cool being over there and enjoying "family" life. It wasn't that I didn't have my mom, brother, and extended family, but this was a family with a dad, and I fit right in with them. He took time with us, and that was really all we desired at this point with ours gone. All he did with and for us and the love he showed his wife and kids made him the perfect father.

He was such a great dad to my friends, or so I thought. I was so excited to be permitted to stay out that I wasn't expecting the night he came into the room and started sexually molesting me. It honestly came as a shock that he came into their room at all, and to see his body drop to the floor, in my mind, I knew it wasn't right. I laid there in the middle of the two sisters hoping he was only coming in to just check on us. It didn't start with me at first, only the oldest sister. The weirdest thing is he never touched the youngest sister; it would only be her or me when I would come and spend the night to go to church on Sundays. I never understood how he could walk down a long hallway, pass his youngest daughter's room, come into the room where I was, and choose me. Again, I never spoke or uttered a single word. The sexual molestation went on for about two more years, and then mommy said we were moving. It was such a relief to know that I did not have to ever see him again, but mentally, I would. Mentally I couldn't escape him. It was torture to think about it. I thought I was safe, but apparently not. Two years was a long time, and many may wonder why I kept going back. If I had said I didn't want to go back, my mother would have asked why, and I was silent about it, so that wasn't an option.

As I got older, I realized that he was a man who could violate the trust he built with his wife and children and then walk away without punishment. He was able to cause pain and suffering in mine and his daughter's life but move on without any repercussions. I just didn't get how he could be so amazing in front of others but do what he did to us. I thought that my family was messed up because my dad was gone but look at what happened when a dad was there? What was the truth about a good family?

If I had to tell him how I felt, I would say, "The destruction you caused was a mere chapter in our lives that honestly, no one will ever completely know about. I know that you will probably deny what you did to me and her when talking to others, but you cannot pretend with me. I am the one you violated. I am the one you betrayed. I am the one who remembers. You cannot run away from me or God. I know the truth, no matter what you tell others or say to yourself. When that chapter in your life was over, and you couldn't touch me again, you moved on. But your actions had a huge impact on the rest of my childhood. Your actions gave me anger that a child/adolescent should never have to feel. You gave me fear that only children who have been traumatized have. You gave me nightmares every night for years. I would wake up screaming in terror, trying to escape the monster in my dream that I always knew was you, even at a young age. You trampled my trust for any man or boy to enter my life. You gave me a temper that led me to be very angry at others. Due to your actions, I suffered from depression up until now in my adult years, and, on occasion, it almost led me to end my own life.

Even when times seemed to be good, a simple trigger would give me a flashback, sending me right back to when and where all the fears began. You took away my childhood. You took away my time to learn and develop respectful and appropriate relationships with others. You left a child with nothing but fear, anger, and confusion to grow and develop with. Shame on you for betraying us that way."

I, honestly, do not know if the words would even make a difference, but they are true, nonetheless. I hurt many years behind his behaviors. That sort of thing changes a person forever.

At this point in my life, I really needed my mother, but my silence kept her safe. That's what was important to me. I couldn't say anything, but I really needed her. I needed that loving and nurturing soul to feel better, but I couldn't express my feelings about the abuse and emotional state I was in. I was realizing in life; we sometimes experience injustice. Everything that was happening to me, I had to understand that we cannot be responsible for how other people feel or how they treat us. It was so superficial to me, and I often had dreams of myself where I had been asleep and cried over a situation in waking life. I was crying to my mother to please save me from all this misery and pain. I'm hoping when I wake up that it was just a dream, and I would go back to the life of being a child and enjoying the life I had before we had to leave my father.

I went on for years into my teenage years, keeping those hidden dark secrets and protecting those who hurt me. I needed that loving and nurturing soul to feel better. I say that again to say that your mother's love is the best love you need to have, but for whatever reason, I couldn't tell her that the neighbor was sexually abusing me and how I saw him come into the room at night. I couldn't say that he would touch his daughter and that I would just lay there like I was invisible so he wouldn't touch me. And when he would touch his oldest daughter and not me, I would breathe a sigh of relief. I didn't want her to get it either, but I hated holding my breath, wondering if I was next. I would be so glad when the next morning would come so I could wake up and go home. I still never mentioned a word to my mother, and I went on for years, into my teenage years, keeping those hidden dark secrets and protecting those who hurt me.

I can remember as time passed, I ran into one of the girls whose father was abusing me, and we sat down and had a conversation. I remember her telling me that her sister was like the black sheep of the family now because she came out and said her father was molesting and touching her. She talked so bad about her sister, and in my mind, I wanted to stick up for the big sister. I wanted to tell her that she was not lying and that their father really did that to her and also me. But I was scared and nervous, and I never told her anything. In our minds, we want to protect the ones we love and just how she needed her father, and she didn't want to accept that may be true, again I needed my mother because I felt she was the only one that could help me.

My mom, being abused herself, was dealing with her own issues. She was a very strong woman. She showed me how to be strong for myself, move on, learn, and use my feelings about her situation to drive me in a better direction. She showed me how the Lord helped her move on to be better without the abuse, but I wasn't quite strong as her. She had the outline for me all mapped out, but I just didn't quite know what to add to it for myself. I wish that I knew how to help her, but I didn't. It's heartbreaking to see your mom suffer physical, emotional, or mental abuse by a man she loves (especially if he's your father!). I remember seeing my mother get physically attacked by my dad, and I'll never forget the feeling of helplessness, fear, and horror of seeing my mom get hurt by my own father. It was horrible, and I couldn't do anything about it. So, I kept the secret from her so that I wouldn't add to her problems and so that I would keep showing strength, even as a child.

Note #6

My Cousin Was A Boogey Monster Too!

At six years old, we are now living with extended family where there were some good times but also some bad ones. I lay, in pain, thinking about so many instances. I asked myself questions like, "Why would she make me have sex with her? Why would she take me to the end of the road and perform sexual acts with me?" I was scared to tell my mother because even then, I understood, in my own childlike way, that no one wants a broken family. No one wants their family to go through pain. I don't know how I knew they would be broken and feel pain, but I did. So, again I kept silent. Abuse was happening, and I couldn't share it with anyone.

My cousins were the best thing that ever happened to me. We all grew up in the same house, so what harm would that be. My girl cousin was two years older than me, and her brother was seven to eight years older than me. I trusted them as my sister and brother, and I would never question anything they had asked me to do. But maybe I should have. We all spent our early childhood at my grandma's house; grandma lived on the first floor, and we all lived on the bottom level. I enjoyed us being a close-knit family because I would never lack having playmates. I was especially close to Aaliyah, my ace boon coon, my best friend, whom I was seldom apart from. As one of the middle children in the family, Aaliyah helped my mother and aunt look after my brother and I, and she had a younger sister as well. I really don't remember when the sexual abuse started with her, but I do know I was aroused by her, "MY COUSIN!" I would think to myself. "What on earth was wrong with me? Surely something was gravely wrong with me to be aroused by my own cousin."

I wasn't even sure of what arousal was at that point, and only in retrospect could I identify what I was feeling. I didn't have a name for sex at that age, but I could feel it and knew it was wrong deep down in my belly. I felt wrong. She would get me by myself, and we would walk to the end of the long road we lived on, and she would perform sexual acts with me. I thought this was ok. As I said before, I would never question her, and again I can't explain or remember how long she molested me, but it continued for a few years.

I was again confused and thought this was normal, so why would I say anything to anyone to ruin our perfect family? We already had to be moved 1000 miles from my dad and stripped from what little happiness I thought we had, so why would I do that to me and my brother again? As I got older, possibly 13, the abuse from Terrell started. We were now all living in different households, but I still had a great relationship with Aaliyah, and I would go visit them 2 hours away. To me, that was the best time ever because I didn't have to be home and alone and by myself while mommy was out working or possibly partying on the weekends.

One afternoon, while I was there with them, he called me into his room, locked his door, and told me it was ok. I was looking at him, thinking and knowing he could do no wrong, so I was okay with it. I never questioned his authority because I saw him as my biggest brother. He took care of me, so what he was asking me to do was simply lay on the bed while he penetrated me, and it continued to happen every weekend I would go to their house. Aaliyah asked me as if it was normal, "did you and Terrell have sex? I know he did something to you." I ignored her and laughed. I couldn't tell her the complete truth, although she knew, or was she jealous because he was making me have sex with him, and she abruptly stopped with me? I can remember the next summer Terrell having to come live with us, or I think living with my grandmother who lived nearby, because he started to get in trouble. He would come over, and the sexual abuse started again, and then when I started taking a stand for myself and saying no, now sleeping with my door locked, he came through my window that night. I was terrified because not only did he invade my privacy, but he also raped me.

I didn't want to do it anymore, but I was still scared to speak and tell someone. I am not sure when it stopped, but I know he did get in trouble and had to go away for a long time, so I was happy about that. But as the years progressed, not only was I a victim of his abuse, but other family members had also been sexually abused by him as well.

Note #7

Girlfriend! Why me!

Throughout my early teenage years, I suffered from low self-esteem. I felt insecure and hated the way I started to look. I was trying to understand why all this ever had to happen to a little girl who came from the "perfect family". Why did my world have to be so upside down? Would I ever feel normal or free from all the hurt and pain I have endured in a short time? I honestly felt I would never be good enough for a man or even myself. But at the age of 15, why was I even worrying about feeling the acceptance of any man and I figured it was the lack of being daddy's little girl and not having the nurturing love from my mother. I began hanging around people who were no good and getting into trouble with the police. By this time, I was just feeling unstoppable because I, honestly, just felt no one would ever care for me.

I can remember going to the shopping mall and being with my friends who were stealing. They were going in and out of different stores, putting merchandise in bags they had and walking out. The last store we went into was Macy's. I said to myself, "oh, this is so easy. I can do this." Once I put the merchandise in the bag, a tall white man walked up to me and said, "excuse me, ma'am, can you please come with me? I saw everything you did, and I'm going to call the police, and your mother can come to get you." Looking back and around, I didn't see any of the people with me who I thought were my friends. They left me and left me to rot and take the fall for everything they had already done. I was scared, and the man came in and said, "what's your name?" I spoke and told him my name, and then he continued to say, "we are letting you go, but you will not be able to come back in the store ever again." I had to call my mother to pick me up, and I ended up on probation and community service for committing the crime of

stealing.

Though I was still a bit nervous after they let me go, I still felt lost too. I was a teenager who had gone through so much in such a short time. I thought that I was kind of unstoppable because I had already endured a lot and survived it all. It wasn't right, I know now, but at the time I was acting out. Nobody seemed to care anyway, right? Also, along with the abuse, I could now add betrayal to the list. They were supposed to be my friends. I tried trusting people again and look what happened. I did not know why it all was happening to me, but it was.

Note #8

The RAPE!

People who I trusted, and thought were my friends, again, were now very jealous of me. They beat me up and cut my hair and threw me in the car where I was trapped with no way to escape. Scared and not knowing what they were going to do with me, I had no choice but to just wait. They took me to the city of Atlanta and threw me out of the car in the middle of the night. Alone in a big city where I had never been, I trusted this guy who saw me crying and sitting on the curb, not knowing what to do. He said to me, "Are you okay? What happened? I saw those girls put you out of the car. Do you need a way home?" I immediately responded, just wanting help and to get home to my family. I entered the car, and I found myself alone in the car of a stranger trusting him to get me home. We eventually got to a spot where I was familiar, and I knew I was almost there, and then he went down this dark road and said, "I'm going to see my cousin real quick, and I promise I will get you home." He continues down the dark road, turned the car around, and STOPPED.

I tried to stop him, but I was scared because he had a gun to my head, and he told me to take my clothes off. He was about two hundred fifty pounds of pure muscle. He put his hand over my mouth and told me, "Shut the fuck up." And he got out of the car and got on me and fucked me. Yes, that's the word I'm using because it is exactly what he did to me. He wasn't gentle about penetrating me. He did it like it was the last thing that he wanted to do before leaving earth. Like I was just something to do. I closed my eyes and waited for it to be over. About five minutes later, he got back on his side of the car and pulled the gun to me again, and at this point, I couldn't stop it. I tried to stop it, but he said, "Put your mouth on me."

I was so scared because I knew he was about to shoot me in my head, and then he moaned, stopped, and said, "now, let's take you home." "Honey," he said, "that was the best fuck of my life, and I'll bet it was the best fuck of yours too, so shut the fuck up, how about that?" And with that, he drove away. I was ruined. I never saw that coming. In my mind, I was hoping just to make it home, and now I was crying. As I saw we were pulling up to the front door of my house, I literally jumped out of the car and ran to the door. My mother and stepfather came to the door, and I fell inside on the floor, and I hollered, "He raped me, he raped me." My mother immediately put me in her car and rushed me to the hospital. I felt like such a freak. I didn't feel normal. I cried then, and years later, looking back at the rape, I wondered what the hell was wrong with me. I remember that day, and it haunted me for so many years. The last ten years of my life had been based on false assumptions that I deserved to be raped because I never felt the love from my father and everything that I was going through. And later, I found out that my mother even blamed me and said I was lying and only doing it for attention. So, I just struggled emotionally to build myself and even talk to anyone about it, especially her.

Note #9

I Felt Misunderstood & Abandoned

There was a time in my life where I lived with a silent cry. I was crying out for help, but it seemed that no one was listening. I blocked the specific memories and images out of my head. I was in a dark and lonely place and had no one to talk to. I knew I was by myself. How could I tell my mother about anything and ruin her life with all my issues? Or at least that's what I was thinking, but I knew if I could tell her, it would put an end to all the pain and misery I was going through. I just wanted to be normal and feel accepted by someone, so why not start with my mother. Is this the right time for me to tell her about all the abuse and bad things that have happened to me?

First, I had to understand why I felt so unlovable or not good enough, how I came to be so low in self-esteem that I let a person abuse me. Only then will I be able to break the cycle of addiction to them and recover. I had to realize the abuse I may have suffered from my dad, mother, and family and how repeating the negative patterns of my past definitely is the root of my low self-esteem. Either way, the root of low self-esteem is as if, in some way, knowing that my emotional needs were not met as a child.

It might have stemmed from that one parent, which in fact was my dad, who had an addiction to alcohol and drugs. And the fact that my mother was so focused on rescuing my dad that neither one of them could meet my or my brother's emotional needs. Our experiences are unique to us, so only you will know where yours started. But try to work it out. If our emotional needs aren't met as a child, we grow up to have that fear that we're not good enough. We also fear abandonment, as we know how painful that is already.

Our parents may have been there when we were kids but couldn't deal with us on an emotional level. So, we choose a partner whose baggage matches ours, and in most cases, that is exactly what I did. I dated and soon married a man who was very abusive and suffered from drugs and alcohol abuse, just like my father. It is even better if they have problems from which we can rescue them—an addiction or a traumatic past. For if they need us, if they depend on us, then in our subconscious minds, they're less likely to do what we fear most - abandon us.

Besides, if we can be their rescuer, then we can focus all our attention on them. By doing so, we can deny, ignore, we can even numb our own feelings of insecurity and fears inside. It's them that has the problem, not us! And it's such an effective drug that we might not even be aware those feelings exist at all. I wasn't.

The trouble was that this was a dysfunctional dance. The steps felt familiar, of course, as you're recreating scenes from childhood to master them. But two people who are insecure are incapable of fulfilling each other's needs.

To feel secure, both have the pathological need to feel in control. While I was 'rescuing' my ex, I felt in control and confident that he wouldn't leave me. But that left him feeling vulnerable, afraid I would see his flaws and walk away. So, he would need to push me away to regain his power.

Now I was the vulnerable one. Terrified he would abandon me; I would forgive him for anything to get him back again. If I couldn't, it would reinforce those painful childhood feelings I had of being unlovable. It would reveal the depth of my insecurity and fears.

The fear immobilizes me to the point where I have panic attacks just thinking about it. All these issues have made me feel worthless. They have made me feel like I don't belong and, in turn, have given me depression. I've been battling it for years now. Battling the feeling of self-hatred. When I look in the mirror, I see no one. It's come to the point where I feel like the world would be better off without me. I didn't feel any better at home because I would have to deal with him, and I felt like no one understood. All I've ever wanted was some help and to be understood.

Note #10

It's Me vs. ME

I was fighting my own demons, and I thought I was a no one. I was wearing a mask and felt like I was dead. I was trying to find who I was and was struggling with my true identity. How would I come out of this? I didn't know who I was, and everything I thought I knew about myself was gone. It's a rare thing that we look at ourselves and solve our life's problems in one day. Usually, it takes time to work through the more complex issues of our life. Taking on our demons is no different. We may want instant gratification, but the reality is we have to earn it. I've found that by isolating small pieces of the bigger puzzle and solving them first is a sure-fire way to tackle and ultimately beat the bigger problem. If you've looked your demon in the eye and you know how to face it, then you will know that demons will try and attack you from the outside. And they are very good at playing mind-games with you from that outside position. When demons try to attack you from an outside position, they will basically try to do one of two things: They will either try and hinder you from progressing from point A to point B in who you really are, or they will start playing mind-games with you to try and throw you into some kind of mental torment and sever your connection with anyone on the outside you may be able to turn to.

He would always say to me "The Bible says that we are transformed by the renewing of our minds." I had to understand the true meaning behind this and realize that our minds are the battlefield around spiritual warfare. Both God and demons (people) will come after your mind. God will try and renew your mind through His Word, and demons will try to pull you down into their dark and evil ways of living in this life. My main motivation today is to get people to overcome their demons and accept the divinity within. Having been a victim of child abuse and domestic violence myself, I understand the need to discuss and bring the topic out in the open. It's the only way people will be able to overcome and get through this situation.

True identity refers to how you see yourself, independent of how you believe others see you. It's how you would see yourself if you lived in the forest in complete solitude apart from the rest of civilization. It's extremely important to develop and maintain a strong true identity because it's the foundation upon which you develop the aspects of "self" that make you resilient to others' negative feedback, self-confidence, self-assuredness, self-esteem, self-efficacy. My true identity was reaching out to all women and children to help them be free from the day-to-day pain they had to endure. Speaking about this situation has been something I longed for, and I have always wanted to help and follow in God's word, but I was in a dark space with a black veil over my face. How could I help another person when I couldn't figure out how to help myself?

Note #11

Now It's Me vs. You

It's a knockdown, bloody and bruising battle that we face on a daily basis, this race against time to figure out internally who we are. My demons can wake me up in the morning, serve me lunch in the afternoon and then put me to bed in the evening. The demons are our truths, lies, and consciences, forever holding vigils over our lives and dreams. We've conditioned ourselves to this battle and sometimes wear the scars proudly. Over time, however, that scar tissue builds, making any forward movement painful. I'm a battered, broken individual, and like many others, I've made a conscious effort to be the best woman I can be. I take this seriously, and I know that I'm worth the effort. I, like you, have my own demons. We all do, and I'm not immune to being beaten, battered, and bruised.

Demons have distinct and unique personalities, just like human beings. Remember that neither Satan nor his demon spirits are things. Neither should they be taken lightly. Demons are beings who have all the normally accepted marks of personality: they possess will, intelligence, emotion, self-awareness, and the ability to speak. Satan is the leader of all demons. Because Satan is prideful, his demons follow his lead, which means all demons have a degree of pride like their leader. Demons even compete against one another while operating in your life. Curses take root in the same way that demons enter. It may be that in the case of some curses, demons don't go inside the person but somehow attach themselves to them anyway. The important thing, in either case, is to destroy the legal ground through which Satan's demons get access to afflict, harass and torment people.

It is often helpful to know the main ways that demons get into people. To get demons out, we usually need to know what gave them the legal right to enter in the first place! Then by renouncing that thing and by determined faith in God, we can command the related demons to leave with God's authority. The demons will be forced to leave. Demons cannot just enter people any time they want to. They need a legal opening to do so. Knowledge of the things that open the door to demons will also give us the knowledge of how to keep the door shut on them. It is also necessary to maintain our deliverance. What is the point of getting demons out if they are only going to be let back in shortly?

As for me, I struggle to face my demons. They keep growing stronger with each passing day. Sometimes, they end up overpowering me. It feels like a never-ending battle. All I think about is a way out and battling within myself. I avoid talking about this with family because I'm afraid all they will do is judge me because I don't have the strength to leave right now. I explain to my family members they have no idea about the problems I have been facing. Everybody says that depression is *'all in my head.'*

Even my mom doesn't understand it completely. I just know the anxiety has just been growing over time, making it difficult for me to breathe. I have been struggling for the past four years with this, and everyone just keeps saying, "you need to break free from him." If you're someone who has been through anxiety and depression, you will understand what I mean. It's like a dark cloud of emotions that sits right on top of my head. Trust me. It is not easy to live with. For me, writing this book has not been an easy task.

Mental illness is a difficult thing to describe. No one word, sentence, or even paragraph does it justice. That's because mental illness (depression) fundamentally changes how a person thinks, feels, and even acts. It's not an illness that changes one thing about you; living with a mental illness can change many moments of your everyday life. I awake to find myself exhausted again. It's the depression combined with a hangover from the medications I must take at night. I drag my body, aching for another two hours of sleep, out of bed and into the bathroom. I look into the mirror and see what I feared – the ugliest girl in the world. She is fat with a puffy face and dark circles under her eyes. Her neck is too short, and her arms are too long for her body. An image not even a mother could love. I feel vulnerable, and I'm scared of being judged, but I know someone needs to hear this and break out of their own dark cloud. We tend to conceal our emotions because of this fear of being judged for what we go through. At this point in my life, I can't quit. I've quit before and know what that feels like. I don't ever want to feel like that again. I don't want to feel the shame, the loss, and the defeat.

But then I remember. That's the depression talking. It wants me to think I'm the ugliest, dumbest, worst person on the planet. I work to fight the thoughts that rattle around in my head. Depression and other mental illnesses change the way you think about yourself and how you see the world around you. Mental illnesses give you irrational or false thoughts, and even though you might know this, that doesn't stop them from coming.

I remember driving to work, trying to ignore the nausea building in my stomach from the morning medications combined with the small amount of breakfast I managed to choke down. My mind constantly flashes back 10-12 years to the abuse I went through. I try to fight back the tears so I won't arrive at work all red and blotchy. But of course, the long drive makes me cry all the time. Depression tends to force a focus on the negative and amplify sad emotions. It makes everyday things paralyzing and oppressive and smothers the sufferer's emotional state.

Mental illness can slow the world down and make it seem like it no longer makes sense. Everyday actions take on the weight of the world, and each thought can seem to take a Herculean effort to create. The effort it takes to blend in with others in the everyday world can be overwhelming. People with mental illness often appear "normal" to others but then barely function when on their own.

The last part of the day for me, and it's time for bed, and I'm back in front of the mirror again. I seem to look worse and more haggard than this morning. I look to the right and see my pill bottles all lined up in a neat, little row. It's time to do it all over again. Even when taking medication as prescribed, people can still suffer from the symptoms of mental illness. While not every day will look this dark, a person with depression has to get past a day like this to see others that will be more hopeful. If you suffer from depression, try to acknowledge your bad days, and focus on the good days that will come. There is a light at the end of the tunnel.

Note #12

Was I the Bitch he said I was?

I always wondered why he would get mad and call me a bitch! If I could show you how awful you made me feel, you would never want to look me in my eyes ever again and call me a bitch. And of course, my life hasn't gone as planned, but in all actuality, he was the one that made me into a bitch. I feel like I had mastered shrinking down my emotions and expectations to avoid coming across as crazy to him. I noticed he was always denying the reality of what he was doing to me. I had to realize that his truth was the truth in what he believed. And although his actions made me feel like I was the bitch and blamed myself for the entire relationship, I realized that his truth was a different truth, and he will never agree with the reality that really is. And this is not a difference of subtle differences. This is his own facts versus his twisted ideas and interpretations. Honestly, there wasn't a day that went by that I wasn't called a bitch; it was never-ending. No matter how hard I tried to just avoid the verbal abuse, something always triggered him to talk to me that way.

I did feel like a bitch only because I would think about my other abuse and what happened to me. His words made me feel super low about myself, and I actually believed everything he would say. In actuality, nobody has the power to make us feel any kind of way. People only do what you allow them to do. If someone is treating you like you are worthless, it means they have no respect for you. Also, if you allow it, it means you don't value yourself either. How we let people treat us is a reflection of ourselves and what we feel internally. When people know their worth and value, they won't accept/allow certain behaviors from people. I started to feel an intense connection because there was a strong hormonal connection between him as the abuser and me, the victim. The feeling is that you need the other person to survive, and no matter what I was in his eyes, I didn't have the courage to be free from him and his bondage. I started to lack wholeness and feel insecure within myself all over again because, of course, it's a repeating cycle that we allow people to mistreat us. If the relationship is causing you physical and emotional pain and is not elevating you to be or feel like the best version of yourself, then it's time to re-evaluate your relationship and repurpose how you feel within YOU. If you don't know the best version of yourself, stay single until you're more self-aware and have stronger self-worth.

Note #13

Poison Ivy

I had to learn what he was doing to me and realize that my emotional poison was created by his reaction to what was considered injustice. I had to realize that some wounds would heal, but others would become infected with more and more poison. Once we are full of emotional poison, we need to release it, and we practice releasing the poison by sending it to someone else. And that is exactly what he was doing to me. I had to realize the poison he was injecting in me wasn't going to just go away, and likely it's been with him for a long time. I had to set my mind up to think as a metaphor. Just like that annoying pimple on your back that you can't reach, in my mind, this one had to be popped.

He was always saying something or doing something that caused me emotional pain. He would tell me that I wouldn't be anything without him. Who wants a woman with three children? No man wants a fat ass woman who is nasty and doesn't clean up. Even with all the negative comments, I always tried to still make him feel good. I would find myself trying to explain how I felt but was always met with a blank stare or annoyance. He was never someone who could see things from my perspective. He could never see why his actions had any impact on my feelings, whether negative or positive. He was the kind of guy who says to you, "I'm not responsible for your feelings." If he cheats on me, he wants me to get over it.

Like any bully, if you stand up tall, take a deep breath and look it in the eye, chances are it won't look quite so powerful. It'll actually shrink right before your eyes. The thing that makes a demon so powerful is the baggage that comes with it. If you stand up and see it for what it really is, it won't seem so big, bad, and ugly. If it's truly horrifying, then you can see it on your terms and spend some time really looking at it, questioning it, and probing it for weakness. And overcoming and breaking away from the ivy he has embedded in you. Think about what that would be like. You've been married to your spouse and living with him for years, maybe decades. You've known him even longer than that. And then one day, boom, without warning, you suddenly find out that your husband is living a double life. As a truck driver, he stayed away from home a lot, and with him being out on the road, I honestly never felt he would cheat on me or desired to be with another woman. But I found out that it was, in fact, the total opposite. He was seeing a woman in South Carolina who proclaimed that he was the father of her newborn child. Of course, he denied it, but I would always catch him privately talking with her and her saying things that just never added up. I had to learn through trial and error that people can be so good at hiding a secret of that magnitude that sometimes they really are not. But other times, those leading double lives do have a pattern of behavior, one you may not recognize as deceptive until it's too late.

Note #14

I am strong enough

Being strong means you actually know what it's like to be weak, feel helpless, feel like you're tired of life and its burdens, yet you still wake up every morning hoping for a better day. You still think positively about your future. Staying strong during hardship requires you to manage your thoughts, feelings, and behavior. Though everything I felt was a challenge, I had to come up with my own method.

I first had to accept reality. Acceptance doesn't mean agreement. Instead, it's about acknowledging what is happening from a realistic standpoint. For example, while you do not agree with things that tend to happen to us like rape, abuse, and domestic violence, you can accept that they happen. Digging in your heels and saying, "I shouldn't have to deal with this" only wastes your valuable time and energy. Accepting what is happening right now, regardless of whether you think it's right, is the first step in deciding how to respond. Accepting reality is about recognizing what's within your control. When you can't control the situation, focus on controlling yourself.

The second thing I had to learn was how to behave productively. When I started therapy, these were the things she would talk about that helped me deal with my coping skills. I learned that accepting reality helps you manage your thoughts and regulate your emotions which are key to productive behavior. When you're faced with problems, the choices you make determine how quickly you'll find a solution and learn how to get out faster of a situation.

And the last coping mechanism was learning how to control my upsetting thoughts. Your mind can be your best asset or your biggest enemy. If you believe your negative thoughts, your self-limiting beliefs will prevent you from reaching your greatest potential. Thinking, "This will never work. I'm not good enough," or "I can't stand one more minute of this," will keep you from reaching your goals. It's important to recognize when your inner self becomes overly worried or thinking the worst will always happen to you. Remember that just because you think something doesn't make it true.

Talk to yourself like you'd talk to a trusted friend. When your thoughts become catastrophic or unhelpful, respond with a more realistic statement that confirms your ability to handle your struggles. You can even create positive energy that you repeat during tough times. In my tough times, I would say, "I am strong enough." Doing so can help you quiet the negative chatter that threatens to drag you down.

Jeremiah 29:11

"For I know the plans I have for you," declares the LORD, "plans to prosper you and not to harm you, plans to give you hope and a future."

Note #15

Meeting Mr. Wrong or Mr. Right

Sometimes, when we are in a relationship, we feel so confused that it is difficult to know whether our relationship is 'normal.' Our gut feeling might be a good indicator, but since abusive people are more often than not very emotionally manipulating, it is useful to have some sort of external guide to help us determine whether the traits we observe in our partner are basically abusive or non-abusive. Is our partner trying to be our Friend or trying to be our Foe? A fair number of people who find themselves in abusive relationships have also grown up in dysfunctional households and have not had the opportunity of witnessing healthy relationships. To them, abusive behavior may appear 'normal.' It is not, and many men are capable and keen to share healthy relationships. The important thing for us is to be able to tell Mr. Wrong from Mr. Right.

I had to realize that what I was doing was, in fact, me feeling rejection and loneliness. Feeling guilty, I made having sex my comfort zone. At 17, I started to date and had countless one-night stands with men, none of which filled that emptiness and void I was still feeling inside. I didn't realize that I was angry and mad. I felt the need to be wanted, but me looking for love in all the wrong places was pretty much getting me nowhere but to the bedside of much more pain and emotional problems. As I explained before, I started letting people walk all over me and seriously wanted the acceptance of others, so I repeatedly started falling for the wrong guys. Now the acceptance of others is more focused on men and wanting and needing them. I didn't have the father's love as a child, so why not feel the love from them? It didn't matter how long it lasted; it was something I wanted to feel.

I suppose I was starving for something that I felt I had missed growing up; affection, security, happiness, and even just some girly giggles. It is strange how we substitute the artificial for the real. Here is the truth though, these men weren't my daddy. They didn't even fill the role of a father figure. A father should never do to a daughter what I allowed the men to do to me. They shouldn't. Should they? Absolutely not. But their father did, so maybe there were no boundaries. Maybe my need to fill the void was another way of screaming for help. If I had sex enough times, in a way I could control things, maybe sooner or later, I could erase the hurts.

If you don't know how to deal with feelings of anger and fear, you're likely to turn them inward at yourself, believing, "It's all my fault." That guilt depletes our physical, emotional, and spiritual energy until any initiative or movement feels impossible. We feel exhausted and paralyzed, leading to depression. I didn't realize that you essentially are the source of your own unhappiness. But I looked for love in being with these men. I later learned that it was, in fact, my own guilt that was very adaptive, and I was the reason I strayed away from my own moral compass. However, just as often as not, it's unhealthy. In my guilt of being abused, I felt that I didn't have the right to pursue my own independent life and success, which made what I was doing feel right.

Note #16

Stop destroying me

It became my mission in life to save my abuser. I was going to find the cure for him and his anger. I knew that eventually I would do or say the perfect thing that would magically turn him back into the man I met. I was going to save him and our relationship. I was going to be the one to beat all the odds. Little did I know that I'd be killing small pieces of myself along the way. There was nothing that I could say or do to change him. Because he was who he was and because he had his own healing or whatever to do. Even though I wanted things to be better, I couldn't fix him, and honestly, it wasn't my job to. I was blaming myself for his behavior because, in my mind, I was already a broken individual who just wanted to be accepted and loved by anyone who would do it. Maybe my brokenness was breaking him further. All I know is that I wanted to be accepted, so I had to make this one the right one.

I wanted acceptance and love so bad. I said to myself that I was going to help him, and I was going to get him the help so that we could be happy. I researched all his symptoms, and I found that not only was I dealing with an abuser, but I was also dealing with a narcissist. I knew from reading the information that it was pretty much an act leading to defeat, but my life was entirely consumed with my desire to save him. I spent all my energy trying to find a magical solution that does not exist. I never stopped to see what was happening to myself during this process. I simply longed for his healing. I would twist our good days together into signs of hope. I would not allow myself to see the situation for what it really was, and I would not accept that these wonderful times with him were just part of his cycle of abuse.

The three most important things I learned from being with him and his behavior are that he portrayed all these characteristics:

1. He always had a hard time taking criticism. One thing about narcissists is that they can dish it out but can't take

it. Narcissists have a super-reactive defense mechanism. You can instantly set off a narcissist with criticism, but on the other hand, if the narcissist even just perceives you as questioning them, they will be set off. The narcissist is quick to respond by lying, being defensive, or being highly reactive.

2. It's not always that they lack empathy. Some narcissists lack empathy, and they are often described with this characteristic. Many narcissists, however, can genuinely empathize with others at the outset. They can be sincerely caring and concerned, and this is not a show. The empathy will suddenly disappear, though, when the narcissist worries over how something will impact them. In other words, their own motivations and interests will override feelings of empathy.

3. They manipulate. Narcissists deeply fear rejection or getting "no" for an answer. Because of this, they tend to attempt to manipulate situations in advance to ensure it will later work out in their favor. Likewise, they often present things in a less than truthful way or leave out important information for this same reason. Things usually boil down to their wants and desires and what they will get out of the situation, and the narcissist will attempt to orchestrate things to their benefit.

Through the research and learning what he was doing, I slowly learned to forgive myself for enabling him, giving him supply, and subjecting my friends and family to his behavior. I've stopped blaming myself for the issues in our relationship. I had stopped telling him sensitive things about my life because he would use them to bring me down or as a source of narcissistic supply. I had to realize I didn't owe him access to my innermost thoughts and feelings.

Growing up in a home with my mother being abused by my father, I never learned to love or respect myself. Verbal abuse was a normal part of my daily life. As a result, I was conditioned to accept derogation, living without healthy boundaries, and being treated without dignity and respect. Because of my past, I was blind to abuse.

Note #17

Isolation

The beautiful times together became more and more fleeting as our relationship went on. Good days for us no longer existed. We may have had acceptable moments but our relationship and the word 'good' no longer belonged in the same sentence. I began having anxiety attacks on a regular basis, and I dreaded looking at the clock and knowing it was time for him to come home from work. I struggled to put on a smile for everyone, including my children at that point. I had my daughter from another man and my unborn son to think about, but I felt completely broken and defeated. My mind and spirit were tired, and I just longed for peace that just did not exist in my living hell.

I began struggling with depression, anxiety, and a generalized fear that I was losing my sanity. My days consisted of nonstop crying and overwhelming sadness, even some days of not feeling anything at all, total numbness. I had tried everything possible, and there was nothing that made this man happy. There was nothing that saved me from his abusive nature. I was completely broken, and I struggled with daily life. I struggled to get out of bed every morning. The thought of suicide was always in the back of my mind. I had allowed him to have complete power over my life, and I had allowed him to kill pieces of me, one word, one bruise at a time. Abuse is about control, and you are much more easily controlled when other people aren't interfering, when you only hear one point of view, and when there is no one else to confide in. You miss out on all the perspectives and opinions that are usually necessary to come to objective conclusions.

You would think by now that I would have had enough, and I would gladly go to a shelter to escape him. Yet, there was still a small voice inside me that said I had to stay with him and make things work despite my mental health deteriorating and my utter and complete state of misery. My relationship with him had caused me to hurt everyone close to me, including my children. How could I cause my two children pain and not find a way to make this work out? What if my abuser's change was just around the corner, and I walked out? Some other women would get the greatness that I deserved, and that was completely unacceptable to me. You may have called this a great fear of mine. I put in so much time and tolerance. It would make me feel slightly mad if things happened like that and I never got my due.

Note #18

The Illusion of Perfection

Some people may never understand what depression is truly like. If a person has never experienced it, then they may think all sorts of things about a depressed individual. The weight of all that I was going through was so heavy. I, honestly, just wanted to give up. So, instead of killing myself off, I turned to sleep. I didn't know how to control this part of my life, so I just wanted to sleep it all away. I would tell myself, "Those drugs you got won't make you feel better, and pretty soon, it's the only little part of your life you're keeping together."

Drugs temporarily solve the problem of loneliness, and this is one of their biggest draws. They start out acting like good friends, creating the illusion of connection, filling up those lonely hours with their intoxicating effects. Like most people, I have always felt like something was missing from my life, although I could never put my finger on exactly what, until I felt happiness for the first time when trying the medications the doctor had prescribed for me. A big warning sign for anyone who knew what I was doing is that I was using my depression and sleep medications drugs to feel better. Honestly, I was self-medicating to take the pain away and create in my mind the illusion I would be better, or it would all be over when I woke up the next day.

The stumbling block is to consciously admit that you are self-medicating. But I wasn't ready to be honest with myself. I would have to consciously admit that something was wrong. For me, addressing the issues and going anywhere near that emotional minefield was very scary, which is probably why I was using the medications the doctor prescribed to cover it up in the first place. But exactly what it was I was trying to cover up was very challenging for me and quite hard to put into words. Unlike physical pain, emotional pain, especially when it occurs in childhood, is usually rationalized for so long that you come to doubt whether it's even there. It flits at the edge of your conscious thought, where you might feel a deep sense of unease or discomfort but can't really pin it down. What I did know for sure is that my uncomfortable feeling goes away for a while when I consume my prescriptions, and how could that be a bad thing?

But what I had to realize is that my emotional wounds would probably stay around forever until I decided to confront them squarely. I had to tell myself they wouldn't just go away on their own. I had to find relief through my own increased insight and effort. Like I stated, the only thing the drug can do for you is cover up your symptoms for a very brief period, but in so doing, they become a dangerous crutch, helping you ignore your serious underlying problem.

Notes #19

My Daughter's Story!

My daughter was also enduring abuse, and me being so blind to my own abuse I couldn't help her. I didn't even know he was physically abusing her. It may seem naïve of me, but I thought it was all just in my mind. Despite everything I had gone through, I somehow convinced myself, time and time again, that he wouldn't do anything to her. Maybe deep down, I knew something was wrong. I've seen and experienced many things, so I should have paid attention to the tell-tale signs. She began to do things that were not normal, cutting herself and erasing her skin away. Her grades and performance immediately dropped in school and started acting out. She was caught on the phone watching porn websites, and she was paying more attention to sexual things. She was scared to be around him. It wasn't until we moved, and she started going to her biological father's house more that I discovered what was happening.

She had a conversation with her grandmother that he was choking her at night for no reason. I honestly was never informed by her directly; it was always from someone she confided in or by a knock at the door from the police with DSS saying they were coming to investigate possible abuse in the home. It was never proven, so I would win my case, and then she would come back home. I honestly made myself blind to what was happening around me because I wanted to leave so bad. How could I be so stupid not to protect my daughter from these allegations that she kept bringing up? But it wasn't until she was 13 years old that she finally told me out of her mouth what she had gone through. I knew from that day forward as a mother and someone who was abused mentally, physically, emotionally, and sexually, I had to break this cycle for her.

I had to break the cycle because I owed it to her to do so. Her story hurt me to hear. This is what she said:

"Every day seemed fun and happy for me. My mother was married to my brother's father, and we always did family events. It

was lovely seeing him and being with my mom. We went places and did new and fun things. We all would take family trips. We would get together on the weekends and cook our favorite foods. Once mom and my stepdad took us all camping at a state park. We would come together as a family and sing and dance and just enjoy ourselves.

Then it all changed. I was ten years old when it did. When he started with the physical and mental abuse, I began to think that my body must be giving off a scent that made people want me and that it was all part of puberty or something. For two years, I was silent about it. I felt like I was being used, like some sort of object. I began to become depressed. I started to self-harm and acted out so that my mother would notice, but she was scared of her own abuse. He would tell me that he would kill me and her if I told her, so I stayed quiet to protect my mother. I didn't know what he would do to her behind that room door.

A part of his abusing me was him coming into my room at night and choking me until I passed out. I would try to remember funny things I had watched or try to watch videos to take my mind off it. I felt upset all the time and would spend most of it in my room on my own. I also became really scared to go out of the house by myself and wouldn't even play with any of my neighborhood friends. I worried that he might be outside waiting for me, or something might happen to mom and my brother if I wasn't at home. I was anxious about school, my future, my looks. My self-esteem was so low. I didn't want to live at all.

At school, I became even quieter and distanced myself from friends because I didn't want them to know what had happened to me, and I didn't think they would understand even if they did know. Even now, only a couple of my friends know. Because of that, I isolated myself – it is only recently that I have started talking to people more, and friendships at school have improved. But I still felt bullied at times. I had to speak about it. I spoke with my grandma, and she believed me. Now the police and social services were involved, and everyone was so kind and, more importantly, believed me. The police officers were so supportive. They came and did an investigation, and they removed us from the home. I am glad I could finally tell someone about the abuse, but I feel guilty for what I have put my mom through.

I started to act out sexually online. I wanted boys to love my body. I sent pictures and sexted to some boys. My counselor tells me that it's normal to do this after being sexually abused as you are used to someone loving your body. I feel really shocked that my brother's dad could do what he did. He ruined my childhood and tarnished all the good memories I had with him. All I can think of now are the bad things he did to me. The thought of going to court made me very nervous, but I was pleased the CPS had agreed to prosecute. At the last moment, he pleaded guilty and was convicted to 12 years with a minimum of two to be served in prison. I never want to see him again. But the atmosphere in the house is strange. While mom and I are happy that he was convicted, we are mindful that my brother is very upset that he would be without his dad for two years."

Note #20

A Mother's Story!

How did I feel when told my daughter had been abused for more than two years by her dad, my ex? I may have laughed as it was so shocking, and momentarily I thought I was being filmed for some kind of reality program. Then I felt physically sick. But I was also thinking, what if she's lying? Why would she lie? What will happen to her?

The guilt I felt at doubting her was awful and could have destroyed the solid relationship we had and, thankfully, we still have. I took the risk of being thought of as a bad mom and voiced my disbelief to my therapist. The relief of not being judged and the realization that it wasn't that I didn't believe her but that I couldn't believe it of him was immense. When he finally pleaded guilty, just before we were due to go to trial, it was like being told all over again, but this time there was no doubt, and it felt even more devastating.

I felt so alone, unable to be open with friends and family, not because I didn't want to talk about it, but doing so would have identified my daughter, which I couldn't do. I went through a stage when I worried it was my fault. Had I been bossy and a ballbreaker when we had been together? Was it his way of getting back at me? Was he mad we had sent him to prison for two years? Oh, don't get me wrong, I will never forgive him for all the hurt and pain he caused me and my kids. I didn't want to ever be around him again. I never wanted to forgive him for the abuse he caused me, and now I allowed my daughter to be abused by him as well. I never want to see him, and if I were told he was dead, it wouldn't worry me. But I am not wasting any more time on him. I feel foolish and guilty for not recognizing that something was wrong, but to be honest, even on reflection, only one event sticks out, and at the time, I was questioning why my daughter was so afraid to be alone or even be around him.

I still feel angry that I trusted him to protect my daughter from this, and yet he was the one abusing her. The impact of his actions on this family is immense. My daughter has depression and anxiety, is on prescribed medication, and receiving counseling. My son is confused about how someone he loved could have harmed his sister (he is unaware of the actual trauma but knows his dad hurt her). I'm on medication for depression, receiving counseling, and using coping skills to overcome this trauma. I feel our family past has been tainted, and I am finding it difficult to remember experiences in a positive light; I would rather not remember them at all.

Note #21

Fuck your feelings

I've had my fair share of his abuse. I can remember nights going to bed sick to my stomach and wishing the world would just end and take me out of my misery. It was no fun. At all. I knew without a shadow of a doubt that no matter what I said or did, nothing was going to change. My abusive husband was not going to change. If I wanted to be happy and live a relatively normal life, I had two choices: leave him or stay and end up dead. You already know which one I chose. I left him, and no, it wasn't easy. I had nothing to my name. Not even two cents to rub together, but I knew if I ever wanted to be happy, this was what I had to do.

I was definitely in with love someone who didn't love me back, and to feel like that makes your world end, and yet I kept pumping love for him. I was so oblivious and eager that I was giving him so much love and knowing he wouldn't give it back no matter what.

I was in love with a man but felt nothing but absolute pain and sorrow. I felt like there was nothing left except the love that he could take from me. My love was so strong, and it was evident I was crying out for him to love me, yet I would get nothing. I felt hopeless because of all the love I gave this MAN and how much I'd do for love in return. I was giving him all the time in the world, all the love in the world. And I was feeling relentless even though I knew he wouldn't give me five minutes when I needed it.

Being in love with someone who doesn't love you back is a burning red pain. It's a pain like nothing else because no matter what you do or what medicine or treatment you give to that pain, it's still there. It's there when you see his face, hear his voice, remember his touch. It's always there. I was in love with a man and tried so hard to love him, and I was getting to the point of fucking hating him. I hated the person I had become and hated that he had ripped me open, eaten me up, and had left me to decay. I hated myself more than I could have ever hated him. I hated the things he stole from me. He took a part of my life that I would never get back. He took my family from me, and they hated me. I was at a point where I never wanted to fall in love again. I never wanted attachments with anyone because of this substantial pain that was constantly there from him. I told myself I never wanted to kiss with love, talk with love, witness love. I wish I could erase his smell so I wouldn't ever have to think about why I would remember it so well.

Note #22

Forgive and Let Go!

I had to realize that I deserve more in life than what he was giving me. I had to also realize and know that being alone is better than being hurt on a daily basis. And daily, I would fantasize about a life that did not include being screamed at, verbally and physically attacked, humiliated, and unhappy. The question is, how would I make that fantasy a reality? Is there even an ounce of strength left inside of me to take that first step in leaving? Should I forgive and let go so that I can start my journey of healing?

I would say to myself, "it is just easier to stay with him because the mere thought of starting over is utterly exhausting. The problem is, if I stay, the situation alone gives me a slow and torturous death. Brandie, parts of you have already died because of the abuse you dealt with as a child; You are not the same person you were before enduring his abuse, and chances are you will never be that person again." What I failed to realize is that I will not be the person before all this abuse in my life. "The person you were prior to this is exactly why you wound up tolerating such unacceptable treatment from another human being. The last thing you need to be is the person you once were."

At this point in my life, I was known to everyone as the boy who cried wolf because I would say I was going to leave, but I never did. I had to have a long talk with the people that truly loved me to know that it was acceptable for me to walk away from my abuser. I could feel the strength inside of me begin to increase after I heard that they would be delighted for me to leave him. They forgave me for the pain that my relationship had caused them, and all they wanted was for me to be safe and happy again. This was the spark I needed to walk away from one of the worst things I had ever experienced.

Note #23

Time will heal

I am standing here today to say:

"I forgive all of the people who have wronged me and took advantage of me as a person."

I had to tell myself things will actually get worse before they get better. And I kept saying to myself, time will heal all wounds. Was that true? I had to wait and see. It was painful and agonizing because all I could wonder is, "When would it all just stop.?" I had to realize that I am not what happens to me; I am what I choose to become. So if I kept sitting around, holding onto the negative energy of all those who had wronged me or everything that has gone wrong in my life, it would take away the focus or positivity of how I could make things better for myself and overcome the abuse. I realized that letting go of the hurt and pain didn't mean I was a pushover or a weak individual. It was growth and important for me to be a better person. By holding onto grudges, it was inhibiting me and tearing me down from what I needed to be.

I realized the past pain was just that. If I kept harboring the pain, it would create a lifetime of pain and bring on other challenges I didn't need to face. I had to believe my ex's abuse was not my fault. However, many victims of abuse are gaslighted into believing that they brought the abuse on themselves. Other victims blame themselves for not seeing the abuse for what it was, not seeing it sooner, or not leaving sooner. While in the process of healing from abuse, forgive yourself and know that you did the best you could and got out as soon as you could. Anyone can fall victim to abuse. Do not blame yourself.

The damage from the abuse didn't happen overnight, and you won't find a way to heal from it overnight, either. I had to recognize that I had been on an emotional rollercoaster throughout the relationship, and it would take time for my mind, heart, and nervous system to come back to calm. Some days would be harder than others. I had to develop my own techniques that would help me, which can help you get through the rough days. Just to name a few, I will list them below. First, you must reclaim control and get counseling. You must recognize that there is nothing wrong with you to get closure. Even more, as you have more and more good days, you will be ever more ready to leave the past behind and step into a new life.

My personal healing journey has brought many surprises. I wish I could tell you I've found a clear path to recovering from trauma and that life has been dandy since then, but that's not how trauma works. I've had many ups and downs and pulling myself out of the dizzying effects of abuse has been one of the most difficult parts. But one of the surprises that gave me the most hope is the realization that I've got more tools for recovering my sense of reality than I ever imagined. I've also got the opportunity to work with many other survivors, so I know for a fact that I'm not the only one with these tools. You can move toward healing, too.

Note #24

I am a survivor, not a victim!

Someone who saw me go through the abuse of being married asked me once, "how do you hold your head up so high after all you have been through?" You need to get out of your own way. You are only a victim of your thoughts, words, and actions. Change your thoughts, abandon your victim mentality and become victorious from victim to VICTOR. How people treated me was not my fault, and I had to take a stand for myself to become victorious. I can't change the thoughts and actions of these horrible people who mistreated me. I had to accept it and stop pretending and realize hurt people hurt people.

Making mistakes was one of the last things I wanted to do after I left my abusive ex. All I could think was that my own mistakes got me in that terrifying situation in the first place. And I still had my ex's words ringing in my head – every time he told me it was my own fault when he hurt me or that I was a failure who couldn't do anything right.

This is exactly how abuse erodes your trust in yourself. When you're constantly hearing that you're doing something wrong, it's only natural to begin to question whether you can do anything right.

Immediately after our relationship ended, I was sure that the only way to recover from this was to be absolutely sure that everything I did was the "right" thing to do.

Except that we all make mistakes, so of course, I couldn't do everything "right."

Over time, I realized my self-imposed pressure to be perfect was actually a lingering effect of trauma. And making mistakes was far from a sign that something was "wrong" with me. It was simply a sign that I'm human.

I didn't want people to feel bad for me anymore, and I had to take action and stand on my decisions to heal myself. I was going to be okay and remembered that I'd been in this place before when I was a child. Yes, I was uncomfortable and anxious and scared, but I survived. To feel how I was feeling was painful and yet liberating. I knew I could get through it. It was not going to be immediately, but time would soon pass. I want to share some of the unexpected things that have helped me recover my truth, my reality, and my trust in myself. I hope you find some of these ideas useful as you heal from the painful impact of abuse. And I hope you can connect with your own wisdom that has already helped you survive and will continue to help you find the safety and happiness you deserve.

Note #25

Hello Gorgeous! The Birth of Kaylynn.

While being abused again, I started hiding and secretly being with a man who was the best thing to me. He did everything my husband didn't do. And yes, I said husband. I was married, but I was focused and happy with someone else. I remember the day it happened. He was being put away for the abuse of my younger daughter and choking me in the car while I was pregnant with my son. I was finally about to be free. In my mind, I painted this picture that I could walk away from him, and because he was about to go to prison for two years, that was my safe haven. The day he went to prison was very hard for me, but I got through it. It was hard because, of course, I was dedicated and wanted to be there for him after all he just had put me through. For two years, I made sure the other kids saw him at visitation. As hurt as I had been, as angry as I was, I still felt a sense of obligation to him.

As a single mother, I struggled holding down a job. I would walk to work every day, and then that's when the man came along, and all my worries were gone. He was the provider now and took care of me and the kids. My time dedicated to my husband slowly drifted away, and now I was consumed with Jamaal and everything he was doing. I remember the night he came over, and we had sex. As soon as he left, I told him, "I'm pregnant" I knew in my heart that the love he showed me and how we had sex that a baby was conceived.

So, I was now four months pregnant. I was still having a relationship with my mother-in-law and husband's family, but how would I tell them I was pregnant without them walking away from me? I needed that lifeline just in case I failed, but I had Jamal's family too. I got the call one day. "Hi baby, it's me. I had a dream last night that when I come home that we are going to have a baby girl." In my mind, at this point, how would I tell him I was already fucking pregnant and five months pregnant, and it's a girl and definitely not his child? I continued to talk with him and avoid his family at this point because I was having a child. That was my reason in my own head to break free from him. How do I tell him, or do I just wait for him to come home in 3 months and just let him see my belly?

Time had passed, and it was his release day. He ended up back in the home and was hurt by the situation, but he accepted it. I was his wife, right? Or was that his form of control, and he would start the abuse cycle all over again? I was still secretly with Jamaal until things took a turn. and he was abusive too. He told me he would kill my husband if I didn't leave. What had I done? How did I end up in this vicious cycle of abuse again? I thought it was perfect, and now I had to file a restraining order against Jamaal and now lean more on my husband for protection. I eventually blocked all communication from him. On March 8, 2007, my daughter was born, and her father, who I thought I loved, was now being sent to prison for the rest of his life, and he would never see his daughter ever again. My husband took the role of being her father and accepted her and loved her, and that's how it was. My husband's family never talked about it or made a fuss. His family accepted her, and we continued our family like that.

Note #26

Resistance creates more pain

Surrendering to suffering allows us to pass beyond it. Mental and emotional pain cannot dissolve until we acknowledge that they exist. By ceasing to struggle against an internal or external force, we leave room for our courage to move through us. Rather than resisting your pain and creating your own suffering, you would be wise to learn to accept your authentic self, your experience of who you really are, and what you are really struggling with. In doing this, you can develop self-acceptance and self-compassion. For instance, when the introvert accepts her introversion, she can feel good about herself, whether she develops more social interactions. She can also be compassionate to her own struggles with attending parties.

People who live authentically act in keeping with their inner experiences, such as their likes, dislikes, interests, and values. They are happier in their relationships and achieve a greater sense of inner peace. To resist the pain, you need to begin by accepting your current reality. Your situation is what it is. No amount of wishing for something different or rejecting the situation (or yourself) will change anything. However, by facing your problem, you can at least begin to address it.

Pay attention to your thoughts, feelings, and desires. Only by knowing your inner experiences can you be true to them. When they are painful, you can then at least find ways to comfort yourself and cope as effectively as possible with them.

Choose to be accepting and compassionate to your experiences. No one ever healed from a blow to the head by hitting themselves there again. The same can be said of emotional pain; that is, self-criticism about some difficulty won't resolve that problem. In both cases, the way to heal and move beyond the hurt is to accept it and find ways to nurture the wound. More specifically, with psychological pain, acceptance and compassion are essential to heal and to free yourself to nurture greater personal growth

When you walk with the mindset that you're finding courage, this carries the implicit assumption that spades of courage are out there, outside of you, for you to find. And when I started to believe in myself and walked away from what I was going through, I was at ease and started to feel peaceful. This very mindset kept me on the verge of looking for something outside of myself, and it went right into the idea of being fearless (fearless is really the new perfectionism). I felt fearless, and I am glad I reacted to start accepting myself more.

By contrast, when you are practicing courage, you're present, attentive, and embodied. You're looking at your life and asking yourself where you want to go next, and what it requires, what your heart's longing is, and what fear is saying NOT to do. Then, you're stepping into the heart of that, even though the fear is still there. Finding courage is about something outside yourself. Practicing courage is about going within.

Note #27

It's okay to cry

Giving voice to our suffering is healthy and allows us to process our thoughts more quickly.

I needed to change my thoughts, and it would change the world around me. As I started to learn myself, I figured out I'm not the perfect person he may want me to be. I have flaws, and I do not come with a user manual. I'm learning this thing called life every day and perfecting myself day by day. I am learning love has no right or wrong way. It's a feeling, and to succeed at it, you must remain calm and engage in active listening with yourself. Listen to yourself and escape the feeling you may feel. I've noticed when you love someone, you tend to focus so hard on what you want that you lose sight of what you really deserve. In my abuse and what I went through from the age of 6 to now as an adult, I realized that it's okay to cry and express yourself. I had to get in tune with myself and start believing God would transform me into a new person. I had to change the way I think about all the bad people who hurt me. Once I did this, I started to know what God wanted me to do.

Loving ourselves means taking the time to be present in our own bodies. Either by practicing meditation or simply putting the technology away and sitting in silence, we can begin to pay attention to ourselves. People who practice self-love regularly tend to know what they think, want, and feel. By being mindful of who you are, you give yourself the opportunity to act on the knowledge you've gathered to make yourself feel better.

When I was in my final years of high school, I started noticing a continuous overall monthly mood shift. My anxiety and depression symptoms ramped up and left me exhausted. Because I was mindful of how I was feeling, I knew to seek a specialist for answers, who ultimately believed that my swinging feelings of anxiety most likely came from a pretty severe hormone imbalance. This is not uncommon but is also not so easy to pinpoint. Once I took the time to listen to my body, I could see very clear symptoms of my imbalance and worked with a doctor to correct it.

It's so easy, as humans, to be so hard on ourselves. Recovery or relief from mental health issues requires self-investigation. When done right, this process includes admitting negative things about yourself. The downside of taking responsibility for our actions is that we tend to punish ourselves for mistakes we have made while learning and growing.

Before you can truly love yourself, you must accept that you are human and not perfect. Give yourself a break by practicing being less hard on yourself. There are no failures, only opportunities to grow and learn. By shifting your thinking to forgiveness, you will cultivate the best form of unconditional self-love.

Through my struggles with mental health, I have learned that I am an important ally for myself. There are some things I can do to help relieve my feelings of anxiety, but only I can choose when to take my medication, go to therapy, or get out of bed in the morning. By focusing on shifting the thoughts of self-doubt to self-love, you can become a valuable person in the fight for your own mental health.

Note #28

The Miracle of You

Once I forced my ex-abuser out of my head (or at least forced him out of a good bit of it), I could concentrate on the important things. For one, deciding how to support myself was scary! I didn't have a clue as to where to begin. I didn't want to work my life away as someone's employee, but I began to realize that being an employee temporarily was the quickest way to an income. But I didn't know how to become an employee! Truly - I didn't.

I found a class at the library and took it. I learned that I had skills and how to document them on a resume. I learned how to look for suitable work, and I followed the advice from the class. I got a job doing something I loved to do and took it despite its drawbacks. I started to keep him out of my plans. I didn't tell him what I was doing even when he asked. I didn't share my thoughts or feelings with him. I viewed him as our children's father, someone who shared their lives with me, but he was no longer invited to peer into the rest of my life. I desperately missed having someone with whom to share my hopes and fears, but I knew that sharing with my ex would only end in him twisting my words into a knife to thrust into my back. I called my sister more often. I went out with an old friend. I met a man, and we had lunch. In short, I overcame the isolation habit I'd developed in the relationship and forced myself to find other outlets for my needs.

About 6 or 7 months after I'd left that abusive marriage, my ex showed up at my house at 10 o'clock one night. He looked sad but wouldn't say why he was there. He wanted to come inside. I had detached myself enough to know that allowing him inside was the worst thing I could do. I told him that I had company, that it wasn't a good time to visit. I felt good. I really did! I looked around: I had a job; I had a house. I had enough income to feed myself, our boys, and my cats. I had friends and family who checked in on me and whom I called just for fun. I wasn't all the way healed, but I was a lot closer to it than I could have imagined half a year ago.

You can be happier, too. Be patient with yourself, but don't look back to your abuser for comfort. When you find yourself second-guessing your decision to leave, think about the crap you used to tolerate and ask yourself if you want your abuser's manipulative behaviors back in your life. It's normal to want to retreat, but it's also normal to overcome abuse. You can do it.

Rather than interpreting it as a punishment, we can choose to see pain as just another bodily sensation. We certainly do not have to enjoy it, but we can strive to accept pain as a part of being human. I came to the realization that even though a part of me still felt sorry for him and wanted him to be better, I had to leave that piece of me behind for my own wellbeing. The day finally came that I ended the relationship (with my son's father, my husband). He did everything in his power to lure me back in. He made empty promises of change, he threatened me, he cried, he screamed. The difference was that I was now full of knowledge about what was happening to me, and I could see right through his tactics to drag me back in. I gave him a part of me that I will never get back. I've also come to accept that a part of me needed to be given away. I had harbored things throughout my life, leading to me being the perfect victim for an abuser. So, he can keep that part of me because I don't need it.

The struggle is real.

I did, in fact, go back to the man who had caused me so much hurt and pain. Why did I become so weak-minded again and allow him to lure me back when we were almost at the home stretch of being free?

Note #29

Redefining Myself! Maryland Here We Come!

The struggle is definitely real. But the struggle can also start the story. It can motivate us to rewrite our lives into a new story. The struggles can lead us to a new source of hope and freedom, and somehow, even the worst of life can become a place of strength and growth. The struggle is real. And the struggle can be good.

My struggle led me to a new start. As I came to terms with and realized that now he was locked away and in jail, I had to move on a time frame. He was sent to jail this time around for driving reckless while under the influence. This was my window of opportunity. I had to escape and give my children the opportunity I couldn't give them for so many years. I had to break free, and I remember having a conversation with my mother in which she told me, "Brandie, the only way you are going to love yourself and live a happy and stress-free life is you are going to have to do what I did when I was married to your father. You are going to have to leave the state of Georgia." Not knowing how long I had before he would get out of jail, I knew that although it was an impulse decision, I had to leave. My brother said, "You are welcome in my home. Just come to Maryland and get out of that abuse." And it was that day I knew that I deserved better, and it was something I had to do.

I learned that there is no right way to feel about leaving and making this journey to Maryland. I kept telling myself that it would be hard to stop thinking about my previous relationship. But moving and starting over fresh with my children was the positive energy we needed for once in our life. I kept telling myself it's completely normal for me to feel this way, and often I felt like leaving the relationship was the wrong decision, but it would be the best thing. I had to believe in myself. I would tell myself that abusive people have likely made me feel that I am not worthy of having friends or dating anyone else, but that was not true. I knew once we made it to

Maryland, the weight of being away from the abuse would make me feel good and know that I did the right thing for my children.

Note #30

Suffering is done

    I knew that leaving was the best thing for me, but was I strong enough? I asked myself, "you stayed all this time, 14 plus years. How will you do it without him?" He had brainwashed me for so many years that I wasn't good enough. No man would ever want a woman with three kids. I was heavily overweight at this point because I had become a stress eater and didn't feel I was worthy of any other man. That was why I stayed because it was just so easy to be complacent and deal with the abuse. I had already filed for divorce, and I knew that was a big step for me. On March 21st, 2017, the judge of Newton County courts had declared me and him officially divorced. I knew that was a start for me, or was it?

    Divorce sucks. I'm not going to sugarcoat it. It doesn't matter if you're the one who wanted the split or the one who was left behind confused. If there's one thing to know about the divorce process, it's that it sucks. The divorce process is the equivalent of throwing your gum out of the car window and having it fly back, bounce off your forehead, and get stuck in your hair.

    This is exactly why, throughout my year-long divorce process, I couldn't wait for it to be over. Finished. People would constantly ask me, "Are you still going through the divorce process?!" as if they were shocked that ending a marriage legally wasn't as easy as returning a pair of shoes at Nordstrom. And then, almost out of the blue, I got the letter in the mail. I was beginning to think I'd never see the one with my final hearing date, the day that would make it officially over, forever. I didn't sleep at all the night before I was set to be in court. I replayed each event of the previous year in my head, wondering if I had made all the right decisions, fought for everything I needed to fight for, and worked to create the best possible parenting plan for our only child. My hearing was set for 8:45 a.m., bright and early. I drove to the courthouse in the same kind of fog you'd have if you were driving yourself to the hospital for surgery, scared, slightly nauseous, sweaty, and shaking.

What was I so nervous about? I wanted this day to come for so long, didn't I? And then it hit me it wasn't the official divorce stamp I was longing for; it was just an end to the fight that I so desperately craved. No sooner did I walk into the courtroom did the judge greet me and ask me a few simple questions before deeming it official. His stamp clunked down on the file my lawyer handed him as he looked at me with a smile and said it.

"Congratulations, you're divorced." Do you want to keep your last name? I immediately said No and, in my mind, "That's it?" I thought to myself before collapsing into tears by myself in the hallway of the courthouse.

That's it. You see, it doesn't matter how bad I wanted that divorce. How ready I was to move on with my life, start something new, and forget how hard it was to end things with someone I thought would be my forever. The finality of divorce, the closing of a chapter you never thought you'd have to end, the change of your marital status from Married to Divorced is like experiencing a death – only you're both still alive and have to remain in each other's lives until your children are adults.

I got in my car, called my mom, and didn't really know what to do next. What does a newly divorced person do? I thought about texting my now ex and telling him it was done. Since I was the only one of us who had to be in court, I wondered if he'd even be thinking about whether the process was complete. But for once in my overly verbose life, I could not find the words to say. I figured he had enough common sense to know what was what.

I drove around aimlessly and decided the only thing I wanted to do was pick up my daughter from her last day of school and surround myself with friends. The day after my divorce was made official, I woke up feeling clear. A weight had been lifted in lieu of the scarlet letter "D" being branded on my chest forever. To say that the fight was behind me was extraordinary, though to say the same for a marriage I once had hope for just felt sad. But at least I was out of that awful limbo that is the divorce process.

Note #31

Our New Home

In my mind, even now, with being divorced, I knew I had to leave because I would be vulnerable. He would psych my mind some way, and even though I was divorced, I would still go back to him because it was so easy and convenient for me and him. But through this process, I was getting stronger because I didn't have him in my ear. After all, he was in jail. With him being away, I could just easily make the decision I needed and leave and go to Maryland. On April 16, 2017, I packed everything in my house and put it in storage. I took what I could in my truck and me and the kids got on the road, headed to Maryland. The unknown was very scary, but I knew just how I could make it in Georgia, I knew I could make it in Maryland. I was scared because it was a new environment, but I had to take this drive and just see what could be better for us.

On the drive to Maryland, I began thinking, was I making the right decision? Was I second-guessing this move for us? Was I just feeling guilty? These thoughts were very intrusive. Then, I realized the answer lies in understanding that intrusive thoughts are actually just thoughts that need immediate and deliberate attention. I need not be scared or ashamed of these thoughts, no matter how shocking they may be. Now that is a wonderful thought. I think intrusive thoughts as a topic need to be in the consciousness of mainstream society. My hope is that people who spend their waking days struggling with what goes on in their minds will not need to fear what other people may think because that is exactly what was going through my head as I began to reach the state line of North Carolina. Time was of the essence, and I was halfway there, so definitely for me, there was no turning back at this point. I was constantly looking back in the rearview, looking at the kids, constantly asking them if they were okay. Do you guys feel like we should go back? They all just looked at me with their sweet innocent faces and said, "mommy, whatever makes you happy. We will be okay."

Note #32

Self-Love

The value of loving yourself is very important for your mental health and to start living a quality life. To live and love are inseparable from each other. Self-love is an opportunity to love, learn about yourself, mature as a human being, and open up to the full experience of life. To seek self-love, you must have the courage to walk through your fear of emotional intimacy and let the people around you know who you really are on the inside. You must be willing to invest the necessary time and effort to develop, nourish, and maintain a bond within yourself to move forward and love who you really are. Going through the abuse, and when I felt like I was escaping from it and was finally free from the negativity, I realized that there were three tactics I had to input in myself to get through my journey.

1. I don't allow other people to define who I am.

2. The worth of my true authentic self is intact, unchanging, and nothing can change it, and nothing I do can take it away from me.

3. My self-worth is not based on my performance or how others think of me.

I learned that people-pleasing is a losing battle. When you focus on self-love and self-compassion rather than trying to get others to love you, you build your self-esteem and break codependent patterns so you can form healthier, happier relationships with yourself and others. Loving yourself can be one of the hardest yet most important things you'll ever do.

What does it mean to love yourself? And how do you love yourself? For various reasons, many of us find it easier to love others than to love ourselves. Sometimes we're truly quite awful to ourselves. We subject ourselves to a harsh inner critic, unhealthy relationships, toxic substances, and self-mutilation. I know how easy it is to dwell on your own perceived inadequacies. I had to learn how to know the real, true identity of Brandie. It's impossible to love yourself if you don't even know who you are. Invest in discovering what you believe, value, and like.

I learned when to say "no." Boundaries are an essential form of self-care because they let others know that you deserve and expect respect. I learned that my battle was over, and I didn't have to compare myself to others. Others aren't better or worse, more or less than you; they're just different. You have value just as you are and accepting yourself means there's no need for comparisons. Learning self-love, I was learning how to be truly present with myself. Our lives are full of distractions. Many of these things are fun and worthwhile, but they can be draining and keep us from truly knowing and being ourselves. Another self-love tactic is to know and use your strengths. We all have tremendous gifts, but many of them go unnoticed. When you're busy and distracted, it's hard to access these great qualities. Focusing on your strengths will increase your positive feelings for yourself. Be honest with yourself. This one can be harder than it seems. Some of us are so good at self-deception that we don't even know we're doing it. Honesty is key in all relationships, and your relationship with yourself is no different. Clearly, you can't love your entire messy self if you're lying, minimizing, or making excuses. True self-love means taking responsibility and accountability.

Let yourself off the hook for your mistakes and imperfections. You're hard on yourself. You're probably harder on yourself than anybody else. Cut yourself some slack and embrace your humanness. Mistakes are normal. Imperfections are part of what makes you, you. Work on forgiving yourself for the bigger stuff. Sometimes we're holding onto bigger regrets or transgressions. Self-love is a process of, bit by bit, believing you truly did the best you could. Today you could do better, of course. Hindsight really is 20/20, which is why it's completely unfair to judge your past self with the knowledge you have now. Remember: "When we know better, we do better." Accept that some people won't like you. That's right, some people don't like you, and that's O.K. Don't waste your time trying to please people who are impossible to please or people who just aren't that important to you. Being yourself means you have to give up your people-pleasing ways and embrace your authentic self. Take some time and read more about people-pleasing so you can see what behaviors you identify with and seek to adjust them.

Note #33

Trust the process

What about "trusting the process"? I stand to be corrected here, but I think this is the tougher part. Trusting the process is about accepting and embracing circumstances, believing that they lead you to your vision!

I found people who did empathize and help me heal. I faced the truth of what had been done to me and got the help I needed to go on to live a healthy, normal existence. In doing so, I learned that it is common for families to turn on abuse victims and believe the abuser rather than the abused. Were you abused? Did you speak your truth, and no one believed you? Did you speak your truth and experience the pain of even one person doubting you? If you were abused and someone, anyone, didn't believe you, know that I do. I believe you. I stand with you, and for you, in the small way I can. Speaking the truth after being abused takes incredible courage and strength. I am proud of you. Be proud of yourself that you can take the stand.

Everything in your life flows from your relationship to yourself. Learn to treat yourself like someone worthy of love, respect, and compassion, and your life will flow more effortlessly, abundantly, and joyfully than you can imagine. Treat yourself like someone worthy of contempt, disdain, and indifference, and each day will be a struggle to keep your head above water. The unfortunate part is that most people never put much energy into their relationship with themselves. They drift through life acting as their own worst critic, working to inhibit their potential and keeping their hearts and minds guarded. I know that sounds dramatic but pause for a moment. If you spoke to your friends the way you speak to yourself in your head, would you have any friends left? Before I started working on my relationship with myself, I wouldn't.

Or, at a deeper level, have you ever felt fully loved by yourself or someone else? You'd be surprised by how many people's honest answer is, "No." I'll come back to that in a bit. I spent years of my life quietly but cleverly telling myself I was not worthy. I obsessed over mistakes from my past. I endlessly replayed embarrassing moments (while somehow neglecting the beautiful ones). I failed to forgive myself for being a human. My journey isn't complete and never will be (self-love is a process, not a destination), but I have come a long way in my practice and hope to help you with yours. The truth of all this is that loving yourself is really hard. It shouldn't be, but it is.

I had to trust the process and ask for help when I needed it. Another part of trusting the process is recognizing when you need help. Help isn't weak. It's human. We all need help at times. We should all speak kindly to ourselves. Talk to yourself like you'd talk to a loved one. Don't cut yourself down, call yourself names, or criticize yourself. Surround yourself with people who treat you with kindness and respect. Who you spend time with reflects how you feel about yourself. People who feel worthy surround themselves with positive people.

Sometimes loving yourself means you have to end relationships with abusive or unkind people. Allow yourself some downtime. Are you busy, busy, busy? It's time to slow down and allow your body and mind to rest. You don't have to do it all. Prioritize what matters most and let go of any guilt in saying no. Only allow the right people to be present in your life. Get rid of the people who thrive on your loss or pain. There is not enough time in life to waste on people who want to take away your happiness. Set boundaries with others. When you set limits or say no to work or activities that deplete your physical, spiritual, or emotional energy, you allow yourself more time to practice positive thoughts.

Accept what you need rather than what you think you want. Self-love is practiced by turning away from what may feel exciting and good to focus on what you need to stay centered, strong, and moving forward in your life. By focusing on what you need, you turn away from automatic behaviors that get you into trouble and keep you stuck in the past.

My story can be your story. We can be victorious together as survivors. I am a survivor. You are a survivor. We are stronger for having survived. We stand together triumphantly and move forward, bravely living abuse-free lives. If you have been abused or are currently a victim of abuse and have not yet spoken out, I urge you to reach toward a safe person and speak your truth. You, too, are strong and courageous and deserve to live an abuse-free life. Stand with me, no longer a victim but a survivor. Start today and make a new ending. Be a voice for those who won't be for themselves.

Note #34

I am confident

Confidence is a way of walking in the world around you. You don't have to know everything, have it all or even be the very best. You must tell yourself that you can do it and stand tall, hold your head up high, and even if someone sees you, they will not know what 100% scares you.

As a kid, I was never really very confident. In fact, that's a massive understatement. My self-esteem was through the floor. I always thought about what the next person would think of me, and with all the abuse and being raped and molested, how would I ever get out of not being confident in myself?

The confidence I lacked held me back in a lot of ways throughout my childhood years. It caused making new friends to be difficult, from applying to be a part of school activities I had a passion for, and from speaking up about things I cared about. It also kept me silent from breaking free from the abuse as well.

In short, my lack of confidence made me miserable. I was deeply unhappy, both with myself and with my life. That unhappiness persisted until my late thirties actually. I never thought I was good enough for anything.

Fast-forward ten years later, and here I am, the most fearless I've ever been before. That's what lack of confidence is really. Fear. Fear of rejection. And this writing is all about how I overcame that fear.

Note #35

Escape your silence

Things all fell into place magically. I still do remember the fear and uncertainty I felt daily. I couldn't believe I finally left him, yet I still didn't trust myself to make good decisions. My entire life was the result of all the bad choices I had made. I didn't know how to love or respect myself. I had no self-confidence and very little self-worth. I needed to learn what boundary lines were and start drawing them. Thick! I needed to learn what love was, self-love, and how to find happiness in me.

I had an awful lot to learn. Unplugging fourteen years of limiting beliefs and being told "you're no good, you're worthless, you're stupid" was going to take some time and a lot of work. I was literally starting at zero and working my way up. And I had no clue where to start. I had never felt so alone and afraid in my entire life. Everything was now up to me.

I had to believe in myself and realize that I am responsible for my own happiness. I don't have to find my happiness from other people. If I want to be happier, I can do exactly what I need to do to make that happen. No one else is in charge of making me happy. The internal struggle that I had to face from being abused and knowing what abuse victims face is often the most difficult thing to deal with. You have a battle within yourself between what you wish could possibly happen and what you know needs to happen.

You have to realize what is going on within yourself, and you have to know that it is perfectly natural to feel the things you do. If you begin to invest your energy into yourself instead of your abuser, you will find your strength has been there all along. You have the capability to escape this life and be happy again. Only you can save yourself from your abuser. As I always say, "You had no choice in becoming a victim, but you do choose how long you remain one."

Note #36

Believe in yourself.

I found and read self-help eBooks online. I found personal growth and self-improvement articles. I listened to motivational podcasts and watched inspirational YouTube videos until my eyes bled. My healing journey was exhausting, frustrating, messy, and beautiful all at the same time. Every time doubt crossed my mind, I'd shout it out, declaring that "I am worthy, dammit!" I did this daily. The more I read self-help books, the stronger I became. Day by day, slowly but surely, I was finally learning to love and respect myself. My self-confidence was growing beyond anything I could have imagined. I stepped out of my comfort zone and made changes that scared the poop out of me but added to my growth.

I completely reinvented my life. I started writing about my life and what could help me in my healing journey, giving hope and inspiring others that they too can have the life they truly want. A life of happiness, joy, inner peace.

I still have growing to do. We never stop evolving. It's just not as scary anymore, and it's absolutely beautiful. I had to learn how to believe in myself and realize that life would open up endless possibilities if I believed I could get out of my abuse. At times I did find this difficult to do. The truth is that we've been conditioned throughout our lives to doubt ourselves. We must retrain ourselves to get rid of our fears and self-doubt to build self-esteem and self-confidence.

Everything you have in your life is a result of your belief in yourself and the belief that it's possible. Going through therapy and being involved in church organizations helped me get through the pain and misery I was causing myself. I was told there were four steps, and I want to share them to help you believe in yourself.

1. Believe it's possible. Believe that you can do it regardless of what anyone says or where you are in life.
2. Visualize it. Think about exactly what your life would look like if you had already achieved your dream.
3. Act as if. Always act in a way that is consistent with where you want to go.

4. Take action towards your goals. Do not let fear stop you. Nothing happens in life until you take action.

You have to believe it's possible. You always have a choice. To believe in yourself, you first have to believe that what you want is possible. My pastor told me that the mind is such a powerful instrument; it can deliver literally everything you want through the power of positive expectation. He said this is the importance of always holding a positive expectation that what you want will happen. It is simply a choice and a discipline of the mind.

"A bird sitting on a tree is never afraid of the branch breaking because her trust is not on the branch but its wings."

Note #37

Alive and living it!

I think back on my life and wonder where I would be had I not left that toxic relationship, and I shudder. My desire to change my life became stronger than my desire to live in my comfort zone.

Yes, it's scary. We all want to know what the future holds for us. We all want answers to our questions. We all want to know that we'll be okay, and life will get better. But life won't get better until you make the decision to make those big changes. It's up to you to do that. Hard and scary? Yes. Impossible? Absolutely not.

You have to ask yourself this one question: "How bad do I want it?" You have to trust that life can and will get better when you decide to take control, step boldly out of your misery and comfort zone, and have faith. Things might not magically fall into place right away, as they did for me, but things will improve over time if you believe in yourself and keep moving forward, one day at a time. The life you want is one step away. Take the step. You are worthy. You are deserving of a better life. Do it for yourself!

Since meeting my husband, he has been the best thing to help me be a stronger person. When we first met, he was like the man I had always wanted. I think what helped us become a power couple is that we were friends first. He would take me out, and we would enjoy each other's presence. We would talk about our future and laugh at the silliest things. His strength and perseverance made me get through my own life struggles. And since realizing this, I've started to use my husband's way of thinking whenever my "what if" panic sets in. And this has led me to another realization about my anxiety. One of the reasons I worry so much is because I don't trust myself to employ the solutions. I always think I'll fail at everything I touch. So naturally, every problem is a catastrophe to me. And that's what starts my "what if" cycle.

So, along with working on my thinking patterns, I also need to confront my fears. When my anxiety tells me I can't do something, I absolutely have to try. Maybe I really won't be able to do it. But most likely, I'll be successful. By testing my abilities and creating new experiences, I can better understand how useless my worrying is. I used to think that it prepared me for every possible situation, and then I'd be ready for anything. But the opposite is true. It freezes me and stops me from doing anything.

I've been in the process of confronting my fears in little steps. Instead of worrying and procrastinating about things, I try to actively engage in solving problems and set myself goals for what I want to get done during the week. When I get anxious, I've been using positive affirmations and reminding myself of the victories. This always boosts my confidence and reminds me that what I'm doing is beginning to have positive effects. It's a good start to happiness in my marriage, and I want to be a better person so I can be better to my kids and the people around me.

Note #38

The power of knowing

While I'd certainly had experiences that were traumatizing when they happened, I was the one who was now perpetuating my pain. I had a habit of hating my life. Did that mean it was my fault? No, I was just doing what we all do. I had practiced feeling terrible every day, and after a month or so, it had become a habit. I was a fearful person. Yes, maybe the original upset or difficulties in my life were bad, but they were no longer happening. I kept them alive in two ways:

1. Through learned habitual behavior and

2. By constantly picking over them to find out why I still felt bad. But I realized that life has meaning, and I had to change my thinking process.

Leaving an abusive relationship didn't immediately change me or the way I went about my life. I was gone, but in my feelings and actions, I hadn't left him. I obsessed over my abuser and our marriage. I imagined conversations we might have the next time we met. I woke to his voice only to find he was not in the house. My heart raced around the time he would normally return home from work. My old submissive routines remained. I continued to fear doing something wrong that he would discover. In short, I continued to behave as if he would come home any second. I lived in chaos, attempting to attend to an abusive husband who no longer lived in my home. Between fear and obsession, there was no place for peace. After leaving the abusive relationship, it took time to realize that I had a new life that could be peaceful—a life I chose, one that he couldn't choose for me. Soon after, I noticed how much time I spent waiting on his next move. I decided that I would no longer put off doing what I needed to do just in case he decided to contact me. This was not easy, and it didn't happen overnight.

I trained myself to wait before answering or returning his calls and emails. I trained myself to recognize his familiar phrases as his, not mine. I purposefully cut his words out of my vocabulary and, probably more importantly, out of my inner dialogue. I trained myself to exude confidence when he would reach out to my son.

The hardest part about retraining myself to not react to his antics was realizing how many of his opinions and actions I'd adopted as my own. So, to retrain myself, I left a laundry basket on the bed for a full week. I lived out of that laundry basket. At the end of the week, the sky hadn't fallen, and no one was seriously injured. I started to feel better about ignoring housework to focus on other, more important issues (like how to support myself after the divorce). I had to think there was light at the end of the rainbow, and I started imaging what the colors signified to me and how each one would get me through all this darkness.

- Red– signifies passion, vitality, enthusiasm, and security.
- Orange– representing creativity.
- Yellow– clarity of thought, wisdom, orderliness, and energy.
- Green– growth, balance, health, and wealth.
- Blue– The sky and the wide oceans, Spirituality (Jeremiah 29:11)

Note #39

Get Up Girl! You Got This!

Do you have trouble finding friends, lovers, and acquaintances? Once you find them, do they dump on you, take advantage of you, or just outright leave? Are you in a relationship you know is not good for you? Are you still trying to figure out your purpose or what you want to do with your life? Are you drinking, eating too much to numb your pain with drugs? Well, if you have answered yes to any of these, just know you are not alone, and there is a safe way out.

There is a discovery to a new life where you can be filled with new insight, hope, and love. You do not have to fight this crazy thing of life by yourself. I, myself, have answered Yes to my own questions, and every time I felt down, I had to make myself get back up, knowing when I was afraid that it wouldn't last forever. I know that the world and people in it can knock you down, but you must get back up and live, laugh, and love no matter what.

Every time I speak that, it empowers me and helps me explain what happened in my mind to myself. I know that I'm doing good for other women and hoping to enact social change so we can change this social paradigm; it's very cathartic and empowering. I am in a good place, and the work that I do to give back ... that's really important, giving back.

We need to help empower women who are recovering from domestic violence. Women have so much to contribute, and sometimes they just need a hand to get into that position. All women have got it; it's just a matter of not being encumbered by violence and fear.

My life has changed enormously since I left. I'm a different person. I'm a lot calmer. I'm successfully raising my three children with my new husband. I never thought I could have done that in the past. I hold down a Research Assistant role in Clinical Research. I'm an author and a mentor of Inspire Me Healing. Eight years ago, if someone had told me I'd be doing all I am doing and that I would be helping other women in domestic violence situations, I would have said they had a screw loose. I'm in a completely different world now, and it's wonderful. I can help women live out their dreams and make things happen for them. It will seem hard and hopeless and pointless but just remember that things really do get better. I have started investing in myself, and I have just launched my own credit repair business to help educate people on why it's important so that they can live out their dreams.

Perhaps starting your day with movement, motivation, and gratitude will not work, but I'd be surprised if it didn't! Will it solve all your problems? No, of course not. But hopefully, it will give you a boost of positivity and a sense of hope and show you that you can make changes that can help you feel better about your life.

Note #40

Write A Note To Self That Speaks Your Truth

Note #41

Write A Note To Self That Speaks Your Truth

Note #42

Write A Note To Self That Speaks Your Truth

ABOUT ME

My name is Brandie Nicole Dixon-Robinson. I am a 39-year-old married to my best friend, Carl Robinson. I'm a mother of three beautiful children who mean the world to me. My oldest is Destiny Dixon, 19 years old, my son is Anthony Williams, 16, and I have a 14-year-old Kay'Lynn Dixon. I've also taken on the great challenge of having a 4-year-old to care for through my marriage. Her name is Carleigh. I honestly feel this is the daughter I always wanted and could never have. I feel life comes in abundance, and I find positivity in every aspect of life with a million things that I'd like to do, see, and experience.

I've achieved much success in my life, and it's only the beginning! Life is about finding new ways to lead by example, even throughout the trauma I've endured throughout my life. In 2000, I graduated from high school, then attended Everest Institute, where I obtained a degree in medical administration and a minor in billing and coding. I am currently attending UMGC and studying healthcare administration with a minor in psychology.

Along with my schooling, I am also the CEO of Robinson Credit Repair. I've been blessed to help many individuals repair their credit status while educating them on how important conscious financial decisions are. That's not all! As a full-time research assistant, I am helping develop new drugs and vaccines that the FDA approves for the safety of both you and me. When there's peace in paradise, I love to travel! The beach is my happy place, and at any given moment, I may be on a beach near you.

I've always loved the idea of empowering people and helping them achieve the greatness they deserve. Being of positive insight is just one of the obligations that fill me with joy. Life isn't always easy but learning to take the necessary steps to your destination is all I want to show others. It's up to us to break those generational curses, live fruitfully, maintain a healthy lifestyle, and live out our deepest dreams! With our efforts and God's blessings, every single one of us can transform into the beautiful butterfly we're all destined to be!

Made in the USA
Middletown, DE
08 November 2021

51405348R10068